A NOVEL

A picture is
worth a thousand
words—and
sometimes just as
many regrets....

The Only True Genius in the Family

JENNIE NASH

Author of
*The Last Beach
Bungalow*

Praise for Jennie Nash's debut novel
The Last Beach Bungalow

"Jennie Nash's first novel is a wonder—searching and true, seared with light and love, wholly honest and good."
— Beth Kephart, author of National Book Award Finalist *A Slant of Sun*

"A wonderful story, woven with threads of a life interrupted and jolted to a new awareness by a bout with breast cancer...This book allows us to see what our yearning for home is really about."
— Sarah Susanka, author of *The Not So Big House*

"Nash writes with gentle certainty of the fact that life is full of uncertainty."
— *Booklist*

"[A] winning debut...This grown-up fable replaces the erotics of sex with the erotics of floor plans, but April's midlife crisis and difficult adjustments ring true, as do the plot's surprising turns."
— *Publishers Weekly*

"A lyrical first novel from Nash about a breast-cancer survivor searching for a home...A sensitive novel that will appeal to many women and resonate with cancer survivors."
— *Kirkus Reviews*

"A fascinating character study of a woman who has physically defeated cancer, but mentally is still fighting windmills...a strong family drama."
— *Midwest Book Review*

"Nicholas Sparks, move over, as Nash writes a touching tale of a cancer survivor trying to secure her dream beach house. Reminded me of that Kevin Kline movie *Life As a House*...but I enjoyed this book much better."
— Lazy Readers' Book Club

"Debut author Nash shines with a mesmerizing story of one woman's triumph, not only over the demons of her past but also over the obstacles threatening her future happiness. The characters are captivating, and the plotline will hook readers from the first page."
— *Romantic Times*

Also by Jennie Nash

THE LAST BEACH BUNGALOW

THE
ONLY TRUE GENIUS
IN THE FAMILY

Jennie Nash

BERKLEY BOOKS, NEW YORK

THE BERKLEY PUBLISHING GROUP
Published by the Penguin Group
Penguin Group (USA) Inc.
375 Hudson Street, New York, New York 10014, USA
Penguin Group (Canada), 90 Eglinton Avenue East, Suite 700, Toronto, Ontario M4P 2Y3, Canada
(a division of Pearson Penguin Canada Inc.)
Penguin Books Ltd., 80 Strand, London WC2R 0RL, England
Penguin Group Ireland, 25 St. Stephen's Green, Dublin 2, Ireland (a division of Penguin Books Ltd.)
Penguin Group (Australia), 250 Camberwell Road, Camberwell, Victoria 3124, Australia
(a division of Pearson Australia Group Pty. Ltd.)
Penguin Books India Pvt. Ltd., 11 Community Centre, Panchsheel Park, New Delhi—110 017, India
Penguin Group (NZ), 67 Apollo Drive, Rosedale, North Shore 0632, New Zealand
(a division of Pearson New Zealand Ltd.)
Penguin Books (South Africa) (Pty.) Ltd., 24 Sturdee Avenue, Rosebank, Johannesburg 2196, South Africa

Penguin Books Ltd., Registered Offices: 80 Strand, London WC2R 0RL, England

This is a work of fiction. Names, characters, places, and incidents either are the product of the author's imagination or are used fictitiously, and any resemblance to actual persons, living or dead, business establishments, events, or locales, is entirely coincidental. The publisher does not have any control over and does not assume any responsibility for author or third-party websites or their content.

PRINTING HISTORY
Berkley trade paperback edition: February 2009

Library of Congress Cataloging-in-Publication Data

Nash, Jennie, 1964—
    The only true genius in the family / Jennie Nash.—Berkley trade pbk. ed.
        p. cm.
    ISBN 978-0-425-22575-2 (trade pbk.)
    1. Family—Fiction.   2. Artists—Fiction.   3. Intergenerational relations—Fiction.   I. Title.

PS3614.A73055 2009
813'.6—dc22

                                                                                2008033890

PRINTED IN THE UNITED STATES OF AMERICA

10 9 8 7 6 5 4 3 2 1

*For my dad, who loves the
rivers and mountains, and for
my mom, who would rather go
to a concert or museum.
Thank goodness for them both.*

ACKNOWLEDGMENTS

Thanks to Jackie Cantor for giving me the chance to write this book and for helping me to understand exactly what I was writing, and to the professional team at Berkley—assistant Carolyn Morrisroe, cover designer Rita Frangie, copyeditor Marty Karlow, managing editor Pamela Barricklow, and publicist Catherine Milne—for making it a reality. Thanks to Faye Bender, my literary agent; Beth Kephart and Kristine Breese for ongoing, unbending support. For a tiny peek into the world of food photography, thanks to the gracious and talented Victoria Pearson; her manager, Michelle Reiner; and her camera guy, Peter. For additional camera specifics, thanks to Doug Morgan at Chadwick School and John Ayoob, photographer extraordinaire. For insight into the world of art, thanks to my wise and generous friend Susan Sawyers; Cardiff Loy, and Edward Earle at the International Center of Photography. For a sense of the realities of putting paint on canvas, thanks to my friend and creative soulmate, artist Paula Strawn. For all the music—again—thanks to my sister Laura Nash. For reading early pages with speed and compassion—again—thanks to Bridget O'Brian. For taking me to Driggs (and to the dream house by the river), feeding me huckleberries, and showing me by their own passion the pleasures of fly fishing the Teton River, thanks to Bruce and Lori Logan. For teaching me what it means to be a mother, and for keeping the secret of the one-girl family, thanks to my children Carlyn and Emily. And last but never least, thanks to Rob for working so hard and cheering so loud.

To learn about the workings of genius, I relied on a book by Joan Acocella, entitled *Twenty-Eight Artists and Two Saints*. Although it is largely a book about dance, I highly recommend it to anyone interested in what it takes to make art. I learned about the photo-a-day exercise from Jim Brandenburg's *Chased by the Light*, and I highly recommend that book, as well as Jim's website, www.jimbrandenburg.com, to anyone interested in the beauty of nature.

Art doesn't start out hallowed.
It starts personal: an emergency.
—Joan Acocella

CHAPTER ONE

My *dad died* at an incredibly inconvenient time, and I have no doubt that he planned it that way on purpose. It was February 2006. His home on the Idaho side of the Tetons was buried under six feet of snow from a blizzard that had roared down from Canada and locked the whole region in its icy grip. There were no flights in or out of Driggs for a week, and once I finally arrived, I was prevented from carrying out his final wishes because the particular bend in the Teton River where I was to stand and scatter his ashes in reverence and mourning was frozen so solid that the idea of a trout jumping in spring seemed to be the stuff of myth.

His timing also seemed designed as a turbo boost for the only other person who he believed had been touched by God in the same way he had been—though, good pagan that he was, he would never have referenced anything divine. That person was my daughter, Bailey, twenty-three years old, who in the spring of 2006 was finishing the paintings she would need to complete her MFA degree from the esteemed Art Center in Pasadena—a milestone that everyone who knew her had been expecting since the day she first picked up a crayon. Just at the moment when Bailey was planning her first solo art exhibition, there were laudatory obituaries about my dad's career, and exultant TV segments about his lasting contribution to American art, and the whole newsworthy question of how we would preserve and protect his legacy—all of which acted like an amplifier for what Bailey was doing with her own art.

And as if all *that* weren't enough, his death came smack in the middle of an important photo shoot for which I had thousands of dollars of artisan chocolate in my studio and millions of dollars of jewels on loan from Harry Winston in Beverly Hills. Chocolate waits for no one, not even death. It sweats, discolors, loses its

sheen. While I trekked to Driggs to sign the death cer-
tificate and shelve my dad's remains until the ice had
melted, Peter, my camera tech and right-hand man,
called the client to say we were rescheduling the shoot
for the following week, sent home the burly security
guards with their sparkling loot, and e-mailed choco-
latiers from Ecuador to Madagascar to request a second
round of lavender truffles, port-marinated figs dipped
in dark chocolate, and triple-milled cocoa blended with
Aztec chili.

I would have killed my dad if he hadn't already done
it himself.

The newspapers called his death a freak accident.
He had gone up to the Grand Targhee ski resort late
in the day when the snow was wet and heavy, and taken
the Dreamcatcher lift to the top of Fred's Mountain.
He saluted the lift operator when he got off the chair,
checked his bindings, and took off toward the Headwall
Traverse. Before he got down to the Blackfoot trail, he
abruptly cut into the trees in the middle of the steepest
pitch on the run, and he did not turn, he did not swerve.
He headed directly into a huge lodgepole pine. He shattered both kneecaps, broke one arm, cracked open his

skull, and then lay there in the snow and the gathering dark, waiting for the cold. But while the newspapers had the facts right, they had the story wrong. The truth of the matter was that my dad was sick and lonely and he couldn't take it anymore. His hands trembled from Parkinson's, his eyesight was so bad that anything he looked at had black holes scattered throughout it like buckshot, and his latest lover—a bush pilot who fancied herself a later-day Beryl Markham—had dropped dead of a heart attack the day after roasting him a Thanksgiving turkey. He was a man who could not tolerate imperfection, who had no patience for suffering, and who believed in the existence of the souls of mountains more than he believed in the existence of the souls of men. Death, for him, would have been a welcome escape.

My dad's luxurious log cabin sat on a curve in the river on the Idaho side of Jackson Hole. It was about five miles outside the tiny town of Driggs, which was famous for huckleberry-raspberry milk shakes, a playhouse theater, and a yarn shop that stocked an improbably fantastic array of spun wool and silk. While over the pass in Jackson, people skied, rodeo'd, and generally whooped it up, in Driggs mosquitoes came in spring, huckleberries in August, the snow in November. My dad watched this slow unfolding of days—and captured it on film—from a house built out of old railroad trestles and local birch. It had huge, open-beamed ceilings and windows that framed dramatic views of each of the three main peaks of the Teton Range. Just steps out the back door, the Teton River ambled by, narrow and reedy, a haven for deer, moose, and trout.

His neighbor in Driggs was Sam Penner, a former neurologist from Seattle, an aging fly fisherman and a competitive drinker. I'm certain that after my dad's diagnosis, the two of them sat in front of one of their enormous fireplaces drinking Macallan whisky and discussing possibilities. Sam would have talked about medications, symptoms, the time line of decline. My dad would have talked about the way the Native Americans, when their time had come, would just walk into the woods on a cold night, never to return. Sam may have nodded, remembering Jack London's famous tale about the man in Alaska trying to stave off death by building a fire. Maybe my dad then asked Sam what, exactly, happens when the body is left too long in the cold, and Sam probably answered that the extremities freeze first, the fingers and toes, then the hands and feet. He might have mentioned that when the heart begins to shut down there's a false sense of heat, and of hope. My dad would have gone back to his house after that discussion, counting the days until snowfall.

He had called Bailey now and then while he waited

for the weather to shift, asking how she was doing with her work. She said they talked mostly about storms—about the quality of wind, the shape of clouds, the color of water when the currents have churned up the sand. She had no idea she was feeding the flames of my dad's newfound interest in violent weather and no idea that he was methodically feeding his photographic negatives to the fire so that there would be no record of his mistakes, his wanderings, his less-than-perfect shots. All she was doing was trying to finish her paintings.

Bailey's specialty was paintings of the beach—its sand and its birds, its rocks and its water, its sky and its sun. That was the view she had grown up looking at from her bedroom window, from our dining room, from our sandy back deck in Manhattan Beach, California. She saw it, however, in an unusual way. Hers weren't pretty landscapes, with children crouched next to plastic buckets or peaceful sunsets fading to pink. She put each element squarely at the center of her work, yanking it forward into a white-hot spotlight and seeing straight into its soul. In her hands, water looked like a reflection of infinity. Clouds looked like something you could seize and taste. She painted with oil on paper in a range of weights, colors, and textures—part David Hockney, part Vincent van Gogh, part something all her own that no one could quite put their finger on.

For her MFA thesis, she was making six paintings. She worked on all six canvases at one time, moving from one to another as she sketched out the designs and brought each layer to life. Nothing could stop her from painting, whether it was a beautiful day, a sore throat, or something with far deeper repercussions. On the day I told her that my dad had died, she was working on a painting of a sunset—an image that placed the viewer inside a striated tube of orange and hot pink, peering out the far end toward the green flash people said you could see when the sun dipped below the horizon. I walked into her studio and told her I'd just gotten some bad news about Grandpa Paul.

"He went to the doctor?" she asked, without looking away from the easel.

I shook my head. "He had an accident."

"Is he okay?"

"No, sweetie. He's not okay," I said. "He hit a tree up at Targhee yesterday."

"He hit a *tree*?" She turned and looked at me. "That's ridiculous. Grandpa would never hit a tree."

"I know," I said.

"But he's okay, isn't he?" she asked.

I shook my head. "He's not okay. They found his body on the mountain this morning."

She lowered her brush, leaned toward me. "His *body*?" she asked. "You're saying he's *dead*?"

I nodded.

"He can't be dead. We were just talking about these clouds." She waved her paintbrush toward her easel for emphasis. "Just the other day he was talking about the way the clouds roll, how they really seem to roll across the sky, you know?"

"I know," I said, although I hadn't spoken to my dad in several months, and never about anything as subtle as the motion of clouds. I stepped closer to Bailey and hugged her. I explained that I would be going to Driggs the next day and asked if she wanted to go with me.

"To do *what*?" she demanded, her voice rising to a frantic pitch.

"Well," I said slowly, thinking that I would have to identify the body, arrange to have it cremated, assure the ski resort I wasn't going to sue, call the newspapers, meet with the attorney, arrange to have the snowplow guys paid through the winter, "to make arrangements."

"*Arrangements*," she said. "My God, Mom. You make it sound like some kind of—I don't know—like some kind of *chore*."

I flinched, because that was exactly the way it

seemed to me, and it is always a shock to be called on the carpet by your own child. "There's a lot that needs to be done right away," I said, backpedaling, "but this isn't when we say good-bye. We'll go back again to scatter his ashes when the snow melts."

Bailey nodded. Her eyes were dry but her skin was splotchy, as if the blood in her veins had been the first part of her body to register the trauma.

"Then I don't want to go," she said. "I have to finish these paintings. He would want that, I think, don't you?"

"He would definitely want that," I said. "There was little he loved on this earth more than you and your paintings."

She began to cry then, silent tears that ran down her cheeks. "He loved clouds," she said. "Giant, billowing thunderheads and high scattered cirrus. And he loved trout and trout streams and river rocks. He loved huckleberry milk shakes for breakfast." She sobbed, then rose from the couch and went back to her easel. I watched as she picked up her paintbrush and palette. Tears dripped from her face, but she just mixed them into the paint, raised her brush and kept on painting the last flash of sunlight as if it were the best possible response to the fact that her grandfather, her mentor, and her hero had just died.

*   *   *

Our Manhattan Beach house was modeled after a 1920s Spanish rancho, with red clay pavers and Navajo rugs, thick plaster walls that yielded deep window-sills and arched doorways, and heavy teak doors with wrought-iron handles. We had wide leather couches, three enormous fireplaces, and sixteen-panel glass doors that opened from the living room onto a patio that was just steps from the beach. During the day, a colorful tribe paraded by our house on a bike path set into the sand. There were runners, bikers and Roller-bladers, lovers walking hand in hand, moms pushing babies, men walking dogs, girls in bikinis, kids loaded up with buckets and shovels and balls. At any given moment, you could look outside and see people argu-ing, kissing, chatting, dreaming, planning, plotting, playing, sunning. It was impossible to be in that house and not feel the pulse of life.

Even more palpable than the presence of beach-goers, however, was the sound of waves booming onto the sand. The noise was constant, and on most nights it was soothing. I could lie in my bed and listen to my heart beat in rhythm to the waves, or I could try to time my breath to their cadence. It was primal and calming. But when I was agitated, the waves seemed to mock me. As soon as I got settled in bed that night, the sound of the waves reverberated through my head like the echo of an evil god bent on causing insanity. They were so loud they seemed to rattle the windows and shake my bones. I pulled a pillow over my head.

Harrison, who had plucked *The Economist* from a teetering stack of reading on his bedside table, reached under the pillow and began to rub my back.

"You want to go to Driggs?" I asked through a layer of down feathers.

He kept rubbing. He had inherited his family's maple-sugar business when he was twenty years old, rescued it from his father's alcoholic confusion, and as patriarch of the family, presided over the rebirth of the business as well as the death of his grandparents and parents. He was an expert in succession planning, which is to say that he was very skilled at mopping up people's messy lives and frayed nerves in times of crisis.

"Driggs is nice this time of year," I said. "Not a lot of crowds."

Harrison laughed. There were never any crowds in Driggs.

I whipped the pillow off and turned to face him. "It's the perfect place to delude yourself that global warming isn't real," I went on. "All that snow, those subzero temperatures."

He lowered the magazine. Harrison was in the midst of preparing to sell the family business before every sugar tree in the state of Vermont stopped producing sap in protest of rising temperatures and maple sugar became a thing of the past—a thing like phones with a manual dial, drive-in movies, made-from-scratch cookies. He was planning his own succession now, and the project had etched his face with worry and his hair with gray. His normally taut arms had become slack, and I noticed that his jeans hung off him as if his body were made of wire. There was a hollowness at his core, a sadness around his edges. I had lately been tiptoeing around him, afraid of asking too much about what was going on or how he was feeling, because it seemed as if it wasn't going well and I thought it would be nice not to make him say so. "I'll come if you need me to," he said. "You know that."

"No," I said. "It's stupid for us both to be miserable."

"You'll be too busy to be miserable," he said, and he spoke with the authority of someone who knew.

I flopped back flat on the bed. "I wonder if my dad will run into my mom in heaven," I said. "I can see her running up to him after all this time, still eager to forgive him."

Harrison looked at me with one eyebrow raised.

"You don't think heaven works like that, do you?" I asked.

He shrugged. "I've always liked to picture my grandpa napping under a tree, and it would be nice to think your dad is working a fishing hole. But no. I don't really think heaven works like that."

I bit the skin on the inside of my cheek and nodded. "I wonder if my dad would have liked me better if I'd liked to fish."

"You think too much to be a fisherman," he said. "Fishing isn't about people liking each other any more than heaven is about people running up to each other in forgiveness."

"I don't know," I said.

He moved his hand from my neck to the top of my head, as if shielding it from rain. "Stop thinking," Harrison said. "Stop wondering. Stop worrying. Just go to sleep."

I turned off the light and rolled toward the dark. "I actually think I'd like you to come with me," I said. "If you think you have enough time."

He leaned over and kissed me on the cheek. "I'll make the time," he said.

Two days after receiving news of my dad's untimely death, Harrison and I sat down at a massive polished granite table across from a lawyer in a Diane von Furstenberg wrap dress.

"Your father did a lot of work on his will these last few months," the attorney said. She was tall, with blunt-cut brown hair and polished fingernails.

I wanted to say, *What a surprise.* There had been a time when my dad was going to leave his entire estate to a jewelry artist who wasn't much older than I was because he felt guilty for dumping her for a ski instructor. If, during the height of her reign, the pilot had happened to outlive him, she would have inherited his house and the millions of dollars of art in it. The previous mistress, the daughter of the owner of the local steak house, wasn't so lucky. During her years with my dad, all his money was slated to be split between Earth First! and the Field Museum in Chicago. "My dad changed his will like some people change their clothes," I said.

The attorney smiled a tolerant smile, placed a thick document in front of us, and left us in silence. Harrison and I read through the will page by page, marveling at what my dad had done. His final will and testament was itself a work of art designed to secure his stature in the world after he had left it. He had everything meted out—every print, every negative that he had allowed to remain on this good earth. Despite the fact that he and I had such a rocky relationship, I got the house in Driggs, a big chunk of money, and the job of settling his estate. Harrison got his fishing rods, his collection of hand-tied flies, and an autographed copy of Norman Maclean's *A River Runs Through It*. Friends, institutions, and organizations got various works of art—his, and those from his expansive personal collection. Although his photographs were scattered throughout private homes, galleries, and museums all over the world, the Center for Creative Photography at the University of Arizona would be given the honor of mounting a retrospective and the promise of forty-two of his best prints for their permanent collection. An artist making such a bequest has a lot of power. Some know how to wield it better than others. My dad was a master of the genre, and Bailey was the big winner of his game. In addition to a fat trust she could tap when she turned twenty-five, she got the best prize of all: he had given her the sole right to reprint images from the negatives he'd chosen not to destroy, and curatorial power over the retrospective.

I got to that part of the document before Harrison. Even when I'm reading at a slow pace, he reads more slowly than I do. So after I read the pages detailing Bailey's control of the negatives and the retrospective, I sat back in my plush swivel chair. The news was, in some ways, comforting, because it made such perfect sense. My dad's well-honed philosophy was that the best photographs were the ones that took the least amount of work. He was a big fan of telling people to drop out of art school, forget about f-stops, and just get out into the world and see what they could see through the lens. One of his favorite stories, which I'd heard him tell at least a dozen times, was a retelling of the way Ansel Adams explained the history of his famous photo *Moonrise over Hernandez*. Adams, my dad explained, was driving down the highway at sunset. He kept slowing down and looking at the sun, which was behind him, and then he would turn around and look at the moon, which was rising full and bright in front of him. Soon Adams became aware of a town up ahead, and then he became aware of the graveyard in the foreground and the white crosses gleaming in the last rays of light. He stopped, got out his equipment, set it up, and without taking one measurement, without gauging the light or considering the depth of field, got off one shot before the sun went down. One.

That, my dad would always say at the end of the story, is how to take a photograph. He would have loved the idea of putting his retrospective into the hands of his twenty-three-year-old granddaughter and shunning scholars with far more impressive credentials and far more nuanced opinions. Bailey may not have studied the impact of Paul Switzer's photographs on America's post-Vietnam culture, but as far as he was concerned, she understood the nature of genius.

As the news sank in, however, it began to gnaw at me. I felt the cool undercurrent of disappointment dragging me down. It grabbed hold of me across my belly and tugged me under, as if it had the power to hold me beneath the surface of the water, to hold me against the rough and dangerous sand where I couldn't see and I couldn't breathe. He could have used this moment to say he was sorry, to ask forgiveness, to make amends for a lifetime of disappointment. But he didn't.

As I sat at the granite table, I wondered, as I had so many times before, if the reality was that I simply wasn't good enough. I could take a picture of aspara-gus for the pages of a glossy magazine, and I could take a picture of a cupcake for a billboard, but capture the whole world in one image? Understand the way that one picture—conceived in private, lit with precision, taken with a steady hand—could get at the fundamental stuff of life? My dad believed that I lacked the essential DNA, and he believed that my daughter had it.

I felt rage at him and shame that I was glad he was gone. I felt jealous of Bailey—of her talent, her confi-dence, her luck, her easy relationship with my dad and the world. For years and years I'd been pushing that emotion down, telling myself that what I was feeling was not jealousy, but something different—a mix of maternal anxiety and pride. But I *was* jealous: of my own sweet daughter, who was at that moment holed up in a room at the back of a studio a thousand miles away, painting the sunset, because she knew without a doubt that painting the sunset was the right thing to do. I began to cry. I just sat there and let silent tears pour down my face and roll down my neck. When Harrison caught up to the place where I had stopped reading, he turned and looked at me, and saw my broken face. Without saying a word, he stood, came over to where I sat, leaned down, and brushed the tears from my lips with his thumbs. He got down on his knees in front of me, then, and leaned his long body across mine in an awkward hug.

When he pulled back, he said, "He did a pretty good job, considering."

"Considering what?"

"The fact that he spent twenty years ignoring my offer to help him do it."

"He hated me so much," I said softly.

"He didn't hate you. He left you a fortune."

"Money meant nothing to him. You know that."

"I'll share the fishing poles," Harrison said.

"Gee," I said, "thanks."

"Come on, Claire. He left you a spectacular house, a pile of money. Give the guy a break; he's dead."

"Don't you understand how terrible this is?" I asked, my voice beginning to waver. One of the things I loved about Harrison was that I'd rarely had to ask him that question. He always seemed to understand exactly the ways I suffered, whether it was from something small and manageable like a headache or something large and dark like the way I never stopped missing my mother. He'd bring me an ice pack for my head, lilies for my mom's grave, and it was all part of the way he loved me. I have friends who don't feel that they're loved by their husbands unless they get jewelry for every birthday and a cashmere sweater at the holidays, but that was never the language Harrison and I spoke. He understood my suffering, which was exactly what I wanted.

"There's nothing worse than losing a parent," he said. "Sweetheart, I know that. I do. But you're not going to gain anything by picking apart his motives or picking apart this will. Take it for what it is, and let's move on."

"I don't want you to *fix* what I feel," I said. "It's not something that needs to be fixed. I'm just asking if you have any idea how terrible this feels."

Harrison leaned forward and let his head rest on

the granite table and grabbed two hanks of hair with his hands.

I pushed back my chair and walked to the window. It looked out over Town Square, with its twin arches of bleached elk antlers. Tourists were tramping through the snow in their furry boots and their chic hats, grinning in the hot winter sun. "You know how you always used to tell Bailey how pretty she looked?" I asked. "I mean, when she'd come down the stairs on her way somewhere? No matter what, you would look up and you would say, 'You look pretty, Sunshine.' And every single time she brought you a drawing, you would take it to your office or frame it for your study. And every single time she ran in a race, you were at the finish line to cheer her on. My dad didn't do those things for me. He never looked at anything I made, or looked at anything I wore. And do you know why I hate to fish?"

Harrison lifted his head. My voice had climbed to a fever pitch by this point, and if there was one thing Harrison hated, it was rage. It didn't matter whether the storm was fueled by alcohol, the way his father's had been, or by pain, the way mine was. Rage to him was just rage, and he refused to get caught up in it. He dealt with it by staying calm, standing still, and waiting for it to pass. "No," he said.

"He never taught me how to do it. He would drag

me with him, somehow expecting that I'd figure it out just by osmosis, but I never understood how it worked, and then you came along with your perfect casting technique, and then Bailey came along with her talent for drawing, and he had no reason to teach me to fish." I sat back down in my chair, totally spent by the effort of articulating my sadness. I was amazed that my spine could still hold up my body, that my neck could hold up my head.

"I said I'd share the rods," Harrison said, "and I meant it."

I knew he was offering something he thought would ease my suffering. I had told my story, and he thought my story had to do with never learning to fish. I nodded, wondering how someone I had been married to for so long could so completely miss the point.

CHAPTER TWO

When I was a little girl, I wanted to be a ballerina because I had seen the pink leotard and shoes of the girl who lived across the street. My mother took me to the shoe store where I was normally fitted for saddle shoes and Mary Janes, and the shoe man brought out a slim box that held the little pink slippers. They rested together like sleeping fairies, and I was hooked. Every week, I put on those shoes and my leotard, whose color was so exactly right, and I did what my instructor asked me to do. I put my feet here and there, bent my knees, reached for the sky, spun around in a circle. It was heaven.

A few years later, I wanted to be Peggy Fleming. I wanted to look like her, I wanted to move across the ice like her, and I wanted to wear a homemade chartreuse skating dress on the cover of *Life* magazine, with a gold medal draped around my neck. When my mother suggested that I could take skating lessons at the town rink, I was horrified. I knew how to skate on a frozen pond—how to race around it, and do double spins with my friends and hold hands with a boy I liked for a few thrilling seconds as he tried to fling me across the ice— but the idea of having to work to transform the raw stuff of reality into the polished stuff of Peggy Fleming was far too daunting. Even then, I had the sense that people are born to be one thing or another—a ballerina, an ice skater, a nurse, a schoolteacher—and that our job was to figure out what it was. If I wasn't already Peggy Fleming, I wasn't going to be Peggy Fleming—a realization that made my adoration of her all the more intense.

I am certain that had it not been for Harrison's encouragement, I would never have become a food photographer. He not only believed that I was good, which was pivotal in my coming to believe it myself, but he did for me what he did for his clients, which is to say that he took my career on as a cause. It happened eight years ago, after an epic argument. He said he could no longer stand to see me so callously ignoring the basics of business: *How much is going in? How much is coming out? What is the worth of your product?* All I cared about was taking the pictures, but he had made me see that I wouldn't be able to do that for very long without a sound business practice.

"What are your goals?" he asked. "What does the perfect food-photography business look like to you?"

I closed my eyes and tried to picture it. "I have a studio at home," I said, "filled with amazing light, and I have a great crew. And I never have to send out my portfolio because all the top editorial directors and advertising agencies call me because they know I can make anything look good."

"Who are your best clients?" he asked.

"Martha Stewart, Oprah, Chronicle Books, Godiva chocolate," I said, without even stopping to think.

"And what's your specialty?"

"Natural food in natural light with an emphasis on desserts."

Once we named the thing I wanted, Harrison helped me redesign my logo, establish a new fee structure that would actually make a profit, wrote a marketing plan, and then sent out pitch packages to my wish list of clients. He was like a force of nature, with limitless ideas and the energy to make them happen. I watched him do all this work for me with complete awe. From the moment I met him, I knew he was an entrepreneur and someone who made it his business to inspire other entrepreneurs, but until he took me by the scruff of the neck and dragged my career out of the doldrums, I didn't really know exactly what it was he did, or how good he was at it. Because of Harrison, I was shooting chocolates for *Oprah Magazine* the week my father died, and was a month away from doing a cookbook of cupcakes for Martha Stewart. I had become my own version of Peggy Fleming, after all.

The idea for the chocolate shoot was simple and elegant: to arrange the finest chocolates alongside the finest gems, as if the alchemy that caused one were as mysterious, ancient, and transformative as the alchemy that caused the other. I was inclined to believe that it was true. There are certain things that pull people out of the daily-ness of their lives—the sight of the sun going down hot and orange into the sea; the sound of someone playing the guitar and singing a song about a broken heart; the taste of an almond roasted to perfection, dipped in a bittersweet chocolate and dusted with sweet cocoa. Who could fail to feel more alive in the presence of these things? Our photo shoot would tap into that reality. Truffles would be set amid loose diamonds, chocolate bars would be stacked atop gold bricks, cocoa powder would be captured in a crystal champagne flute. Through light made to flash at just the right moment, light made to shine in just the right direction, light made to highlight the texture, shape, and color of the gems and the confections, we would make people pause—if only for the thirty seconds it might take to gaze at a page in a magazine—and we would make them remember that they are alive.

Chocolate is notoriously difficult to shoot. You can get three or four shots off, at most, before it starts to sweat under the lights. There's not a whole lot of room for error. We had the whole thing sketched out on storyboards, but since we had rescheduled the shoot to accommodate my jaunt to Driggs, we only had the jewels for two days instead of the original four. We had to move particularly fast.

The whole crew was in the studio on the designated morning, waiting for the jewels to arrive. Peter was in charge of all the equipment, from cameras to computers. Digital photography had become so high-tech, and the equipment so expensive, that managing it was a separate profession. I owned a Canon G9 pocket rocket for family photos and scouting work, but I made my living on the $80,000 Hasselblad H1 medium-format camera kit that Peter brought to my studio whenever we had a job. For the chocolate shoot, we had Ramie working on props, and a food stylist named Francesca, with whom I had recently worked on a Martha Stewart picnic feature story for which we'd taken three shots a day for three straight days and every meal was a feast fit for kings. The magazine that had hired me to do the chocolate shoot had sent out a creative director named Susannah, who knew exactly how she wanted to position each shot in relation to the headlines and copy block. She had a binder with page-long descriptions of mood, layouts, and color swatches to guide the stylists. When the truck arrived with the diamonds, rubies, and gold dust, we all walked from the studio out to the street as the two guards, guns at their hips, brought in the briefcase filled with gems.

"It's like a Bond movie right in your own backyard," Peter said.

I made myself laugh because I understood that his comment was meant to strike a note of levity in a week that had been fairly grim, but my voice sounded weak. My eyes were heavy with exhaustion. I was no longer sure that I could make anything magic out of a bunch of baubles and candy.

I followed the guards back to the studio, and drank another cup of coffee while Francesca and Ramie set up the first shot. We were going to start with the lavender truffle set on top of a pile of diamonds. We had a glass-topped table positioned against a window getting nice light from the west. Francesca opened a black velvet pouch filled with loose diamonds and carefully poured them onto the glass so that they formed a mound. Using a pair of tongs, she made a flat platform on the top of the mound, and rearranged individual stones so that their biggest facets were facing either out or in. She worked quickly, deliberately. We discussed the height of the pile, the width of it, and the way individual diamonds were arranged. When we were satisfied, Ramie brought a piece of chocolate from the kitchen to stand in for the hero—the truffle she had decided had the best shape, the best sheen, the best overall aesthetics. I walked over and looked through the Hasselblad at the stand-in truffle on its throne. "Don't ever let anyone take your portrait with one of these babies," I said to the guards, who were standing at the door and watching my every move. "You'll see every wrinkle."

"How's it look?" Peter asked. He wore a bandana tied around his head, cargo shorts, and leather flip-flops that looked as if they'd been worn to hike the Himalayas. If he wasn't behind a camera, Peter was in the ocean. Those were his only two states of being, so far as I knew, and they brought him equal measures of peace. Peace is something you need on a photo shoot, because peaceful people have patience. What you're trying to do, after all, is capture the elusive qualities of food and light, and it takes an enormous amount of patience when things melt or droop or a cloud moves across the sky. I don't surf, but I understand that the best surfers are the most patient. They wait for the right day, wait for the right wave. It's as much about waiting as it is about riding the wave, as much about waiting as it is about setting up a shot, and this was something Peter innately understood. I constantly gave thanks that there happened to be no weather in Los Angeles on the day I took a Nikon workshop on digital technology. Peter never would have showed up if the surfing had been good, and without Peter, I wouldn't be half the photographer I had become.

I peered through the lens, blinked—and froze. The image looked all wrong, but I couldn't figure out why. Normally, I could read the light as if it were poetry. I could feel the rhythm, sense where it slowed and gathered and where it spilled over into exuberant joy. I could pinpoint exactly where light needed to be added or taken away, bent or colored. But that day, all I saw was a pile of diamonds and a piece of overpriced sugar.

I took a deep breath and forced myself to consider each part of the scene as if I had a checklist—check direction of light, check intensity of light, check color of light, check shadows. It was all I could think to do— but as soon as I started, I could hear my dad commanding me to stop *thinking* so much, and that, in turn, only made me start thinking even more. "There's a shadow on the right I don't like," I said tentatively. Jim, my assistant, leaped into action as if the words I spoke had been gospel. He moved in a C-stand, clamped on a black flag, and positioned it until the shadow disappeared. I looked through the camera again and shook my head. Something was wrong, but what was it? My crew was poised, waiting for me to speak.

"I need some foil on the left," I said, just to see what they might do. They had, after all, been working with me for many years. There was a chance they could read my mind, even if all the cylinders in my mind weren't firing. Jim moved, Peter moved, and within moments, there was another C-stand, a piece of foil wrapped around cardboard, a beam of light directed just so. I took a short, sharp little breath of panic—to think that they had so much trust in me!—and then looked at the image on Peter's computer screen. I blinked. Would this arrangement of chocolate and light create an image that looked good enough to eat?

I had no idea.

I turned to Peter and, as casually as I was able, asked, "What do you think?"

We stood together in front of the computer screen he'd hooked up to the camera. The image appeared there, just as it would appear on the page. "It looks good," he said.

"You want the hero, then?" Francesca asked.

"Sure," I said, and then, "No, wait!" I remembered watching my dad sort through slides one summer when I was in high school. He held each one up to the window, took a quick look, and either placed it on the table in front of him or tossed it toward a metal trash can positioned at his feet. One glance, and he knew whether a slide was worthy of being developed or destined for the trash. I picked up his castoffs and held them up to the light to see if I could see the flaws, but every single image looked identical to me, and identical to the slides on the table. Each one showed a single rolling hill with a black oak tree spread out in the sunlight, its branches reaching toward the four corners of the earth. I could discern no difference between the winners and the losers. My dad tried to show me what he was seeing, and when I said I didn't understand, he barked at me, "Look at the color of the light, for God's sake."

"Wait a second," I said to my crew. I bent and looked

through the viewfinder again. "I'm afraid the light looks a little lemony. I'd like to see a red filter." I stepped back and chewed a small piece of skin that had come loose on the side of my pinkie nail while Jim jumped up and arranged the filter.

I shot a few frames and then we gathered around the big screen again to see how it looked.

"I don't know," I said. "Something's not right." Ramie took the opportunity to discard the first stand-in truffle and bring out another. Francesca and Susannah gamely tried to find something to fix, and decided that one of the diamonds in the front of the pile was too prominent. They went back to the display and, with a pair of tweezers, turned the errant gem a few degrees to the left.

"Let's try a green filter," I said.

Jim made the switch, but when I looked at the shot, the diamonds seemed slightly cloudy, as if they were made of paste.

"Does the light look cloudy to you?" I asked Peter.

He shook his head.

"You?" I said to Susannah.

"No," she said, "but you're the master."

Was I? I wasn't so sure. Perhaps my dad had been right all along. Perhaps light was beyond my knowing. I was supposed to be the one who made the decisions on set, who made the products look good, who understood the light, but I took a deep breath and decided that if something was really wrong with this shot, Peter and Jim and Susannah would be seeing it, too.

"Okay," I said to Ramie, who was poised to usher in more chocolate. "Let's bring out the hero."

It was a gorgeous thing—a one-by-one-inch dark chocolate square with an intricate white lattice along the top, a crystallized light purple flower bud unfurled in the center, and tiny beads of a darker chocolate punctuating the sides. It looked like a piece of the Taj Mahal, but it was, in fact, a product of a Vermont confectioner who used milk from cows raised on organic grasses and Valrhona chocolate from France mixed with homegrown lavender. Francesca used flat tongs to set the truffle on top of the diamonds, but when I looked through the viewfinder, I saw a tiny hair on one of the gems—a strand of blond. There was dust in the air, there was lint on the diamonds. Instead of getting the shot, I grabbed a bottle of compressed air, reached through all the flags and the foils on their C-stands, and gently blew the diamonds clean. Thirty seconds ticked by, perhaps forty. "Try now," I said to Peter, who had stepped into position at the viewfinder when I'd given up the post. He bent to look through the camera, but instead of pressing the shutter, he stood up and shook his head.

I looked at our tableau. The truffle had started to glisten in the hot lights. Tiny beads of condensation had broken out on its lacy surface, as if the chocolate, too, had become nervous.

"Shit," I said. I saw Francesca catch Jim's eye and raise her eyebrows. I saw Susannah turn away from the computer screen and from me. I wanted to scream at them all to shut up, but they hadn't said a word.

"Ramie!" I called. "Bring another hero."

Things went wrong all morning. By the time we had the second hero arranged, the light had changed. It was too sharp, too close to high noon. We pushed the truffle shot into the afternoon, finally getting it around two. Susannah was on her cell phone to her team in New York, speaking softly, reporting the bad news, and that was even before we started on the gold bricks and chocolate bars three hours late. I'd thought I'd be able to make up time. Limit the reflection on the gold bars. Light them softly. Set an angle slightly below them. But the bars of chocolate looked as flat and dull as an ordinary Hershey bar you'd buy for a dollar at the grocery store. No matter how I changed the lighting—added it, took it away, focused it, or diffused it—the chocolate looked lifeless. The whole point of taking a photograph of something edible is that you want the viewer's mouth to water. You want it to look irresistible, luscious, primed for a celebration. Everything in my studio that day looked like it would taste like cardboard.

By the time the guards carted away the jewelry for the night, the air in the studio was brittle. It felt like it might crack. No one would look at me. I sent them all home.

Back at the house, I got a bottle of chardonnay from the fridge and walked into the living room, where Harrison was watching the Lakers game. Kobe and his teammates were chasing the Utah Jazz, and the crowd in the Staples Center was going crazy.

"Marisol said the phone rang off the hook today," Harrison said. "She left the messages in a stack in the study. The museum wants you to approve a press release, reporters want comments, and everyone wants to know about Bailey and the retrospective."

"I heard that," Bailey yelled from the kitchen.

I gulped my wine, waiting for it to numb me.

"Heard what?" Harrison yelled back.

Bailey came and stood in the doorway. She was eating leftover chicken out of a Tupperware container. "I heard you talking about me."

"Did you see all the messages from Marisol?"

"Yeah," she said. "I talked to one reporter today from

the *Denver Post*. She asked if I had any ideas about the retrospective."

"What did you say?" I asked.

"That we were still grieving and weren't ready to make any comments."

"That's good," I said. "Good for you."

"Well, they're so rude," Bailey said. "I mean, he was my *grandfather*. He just *died* and they want me to tell them how we're going to *honor* him?"

"It's just their job," Harrison said. "You can't blame them for doing their jobs."

"But it's our *family*," Bailey complained.

"Our family happens to a have a public figure in it," Harrison said. "Which changes the rules of the game. The reporters are going to call. It's up to us to figure out how we want to respond."

"Or not," I said.

"Not respond?" Bailey asked, turning to look at me. "Is that a choice?"

"A bad one," Harrison said.

"Why is it bad?"

"Because if you don't secure his legacy the way you want it secured, other people will do it for you."

"That's a good point," Bailey said.

"That's the business-school professor talking," I said.

"Think of what Jackie O did in the forty-eight hours

after JFK was shot," Harrison said. "She orchestrated a brilliant public relations campaign with some of the most potent imagery this nation has ever seen. She had an amazing instinct for how to secure his legacy." He turned to look at me. "Don't you remember watching that unfold on TV? I was thirteen. I had never seen an adult cry before."

I nodded. The assassination happened not long before my dad left us for the first time. I was ten years old. When the news came about JFK—a knock on the classroom door, hushed voices, a dark rush of fear—my teacher, Mrs. Hutchinson, sent all the kids home from school in the middle of the day. When I got home, my mom was sitting in front of the television set with some of the neighbor wives. She was wearing her office uniform—a sweater set, a plaid skirt, sensible navy-blue pumps—and her face looked as if it had been carved from stone. I dropped my book bag and slipped onto my knees on the rug beside my mother's chair. She pulled me to her in a desperate hug, but she didn't cry. Her face remained dry. The next morning when I came out to the kitchen for breakfast, she was listening to the radio while she scrambled eggs for my dad. She had done her hair, put on makeup. She would forge ahead, just like Jackie.

"My mother was made of some pretty strong stuff," I said. "She didn't cry."

"I have to finish one more painting," Bailey said, turning to go. "I don't have time for reminiscing."

"I thought you were done," I said.

"The seagull is totally fighting me," she said. "I can't get it right. It's making me crazy."

"Do you guys mind?" Harrison asked. "I can't hear the game."

I nodded, and reached out my hand to squeeze Bailey's in solidarity. "I feel the same way about chocolate," I said quietly.

I poured myself another glass of wine, downed it, and then got up to go to bed. I stopped in the middle of the stairway and looked out into the night. In front of me was the black expanse of beach. To my left was the narrow-walk street that ran straight back from the sand and up a small hill. On holidays, all the neighbors would sit out in the gardens and on the decks that fronted the carless little avenue and we would share cold beer and well-seasoned burgers and the happy feeling of living in such a special place—steps from the sand, in a town that still felt like a village, in houses designed as much for their beauty as for their function. Mrs. Jenkins, the silver-haired neighbor directly across from us, would come out on those evenings with platters of veal and a bottle of wine. She had been an opera singer who was the toast of the town from La Scala to Los Angeles, and Barolo and veal Milanese was as down-home as she would ever get. I looked across at her home, dark like all the others, and wondered if she had ever stood in the wings of an opera house, doubting whether or not she could produce the right notes when she opened her mouth to sing.

CHAPTER THREE

When I *woke* up, I pulled on some jeans and a white T-shirt, dragged a brush through my hair, ate a banana, and forced myself to walk back out to the studio to shoot the walnut fudge made in Scotland by monks who lived in a centuries-old abbey. There was no emotion behind the pictures—no desire, no lust, nothing. It seemed to me as if anyone could take the rest of the chocolate pictures. Francesca, Ramie, Peter. I even imagined stepping back and inviting one of the burly bodyguards to look at the shots we were setting up. He could stand there, look through the viewfinder at the perfectly arranged and perfectly lit tableau, and snap a photograph. Why was I the one being paid? Why would my name be on the credit?

While we waited for the photos to be approved by Susannah's people in New York, the rest of the crew sat down on the couches in the studio, turned up Rascal Flatts, and began to argue about what qualified as a country classic. I went to the bathroom, but instead of going back to join them, I turned in the other direction to see what Bailey was doing.

She worked in a room at the back of my studio, which was a converted guesthouse behind our home. Her room was large and bright, and if she needed to look at sand or dip her toes in the water for inspiration, she only had to walk through the studio, stroll through the garden, and slip around the house to the beach. When she left her student apartment in Pasadena to come to work on the paintings for her master's thesis, she had brought home a duffel bag of clothes, and a truckload of supplies from Pearl Paint—canvases, toolboxes jammed with brushes, boxes of pigment and primer. I liked having her there. She'd gotten her undergraduate degree in a New England town that was a long plane ride away from us and her return was like an unexpected bonus, a chance for us to enjoy the adult that she had become before she went back out into the world.

There were French doors in Bailey's studio that opened onto a small garden along the back fence. Two teak chairs sat under a lemon-yellow umbrella and a mosaic fountain in the shape of a gleeful octopus bubbled and sang. Bailey's paints and brushes were set out on restaurant supply shelves, so that if someone wasn't paying attention when they walked from my space at the front of the studio to hers at the back, they might think that those tubs held neon colors of frosting or pureed soups waiting to be photographed. Every once in a while, Bailey would invite me to come back to her room to look at a certain color of purple she was using for the water or to brainstorm where the edge of a painting should fall across an image. She didn't really need my advice; her invitation had more to do with the inherent solitude of being a painter than it did with issues of design. I usually only went when asked.

I didn't start taking photographs seriously until I was thirty-eight years old, and I often wondered what I might have learned if I'd started as young as she did— if someone had given me space, given me permission, given me encouragement. I gave those things to Bailey like a sacrament; I gave her those things like daily bread. They say that all the great dancers start their training very young because it's the only time you can really learn how to move the body, the only time you can really cement the rhythms in your muscles. They say the same thing about learning a language. Maybe starting young was the only way you could really learn how to see, as well.

When she saw me in the doorway, she looked up. "I hate this bird," she said.

The seagull was flying at the viewer through a hot blue high-noon sky. The profile of its face took up almost the entire canvas—a black-and-white eye above a tangerine beak amid saffron feathers flattened by the wind. You got a sense of how that bird soared, of how it would dip and spin just for the sheer joy of being alive and able to fly. You felt like you were suspended in mid-air, flying alongside it, drenched as it was by the sun. It was spectacular. It looked to me to be perfect—perfect in concept, perfect in execution. "Bailey, it's beautiful. What's to hate?"

"The eye's all wrong. I wanted to show glee, you know? It just looks surprised."

"Why don't you leave it awhile? Come back to it later?"

"If I don't get everything up to Pasadena this week-end, I'll be the only student in the history of Art Center to have a blank wall at her MFA exhibition."

She had her laptop open on the table. It was zoomed in on an eye of a bird. It looked like she had a dozen other photos stacked up behind it. Her sketch pad was there, too, filled with circles and ovals and swirls. I scanned the images and pointed to one. "What about extending the white like you did here?"

"I was thinking about that," she said, and when she looked at me, her eyes were filled with tears. "But what I'd really like to do is call Grandpa and just talk to him about it, you know? Brainstorm with him? I miss him so much."

"I know," I said. "I know."

She brushed away her tears, picked up a paintbrush with a tiny bristled head, and turned her attention away from me and back to her easel. I could feel the shift in her attention like the wind changing direction from West to East. For one brief moment, everything was aligned toward me, and the next, everything pointed away from me, and Bailey was gone, disappeared into her work. She would have just said that she was concentrating, but there was something more to it than that. It was like she went to a different zone, a different plane, a place where the rules of time and space didn't work in exactly the same way.

There had been a time when Harrison and I worried about Bailey's tendency to zone out in this way.

Her teachers used to call us in to talk about her unusual behavior. It was a ritual we came to count on each September. About three weeks after school started, after the classes had settled down and the routine of the year was in full swing, we would get a call from a teacher who wanted to talk to us about Bailey. They'd show us her worksheets with doodles all over the margins—elaborate spirals and suns and houses she had made when she should have been making the alphabet or practicing 2 + 2. In second grade, the margins became too confining, so she started filling up the classroom's scrap paper. She drew as many as twenty princesses a day—princesses in pink and princesses in purple, princesses with tiaras and princesses with long red hair. Flipping through the drawings was like watching a Polaroid come to life. At first, the princesses were stick figures with triangle dresses, but soon they were given bodies with weight, and then bodies with shape. By the start of third grade, they had fingers on their hands, noses in perspective, shadows at their hips—and yet she couldn't recite her math facts in the allotted time, and at recess, she sat on the grass and drew the ladybugs she found there rather than playing foursquare or jump rope with the other girls.

"We'd like to have her tested," her third-grade teacher said. Tested for a hearing problem, a glitch in her ability to process information, a hole in her cognitive development, some defect that could be fixed. We nodded our assent. I was working long days downtown and Harrison was teaching up at the business school at UCLA. Our housekeeper, Marisol, was the one who kept our lives consistent—laundry done on Tuesdays and Thursdays, dinner on the table at seven. Even when we built the studio out back and I began to work just steps from the house, I used to think of Marisol as a giant tree, roots reaching into the sandy soil of our home, arms reaching toward the sun. Bailey had always enjoyed the calming influence of Marisol's reign—the green chili chicken soup made with limes picked from the backyard, the insistence that it was time to sit down and do homework, the stacks of neatly folded sweatshirts and blue jeans—so it seemed logical to think that if she wasn't thriving, the cause would be something that could be found in a simple test, something physical, something tangible, a wire crossed in a less-than-perfect way.

Nothing, however, was found. Nothing that could be fixed. Bailey continued to doodle all day in school and to drive friends away because she always turned a party into a chance to color and a day at the beach into an opportunity to draw. When she was in fourth grade, we went to school one day for a play about the California missions. Bailey was playing the part of a minor friar, and would speak some lines about planting corn. I'd left work early to make sure I would be on time for the performance and showed up at the school with ten minutes to spare. I waited for Harrison at the top of a grassy hill that overlooked the playground and watched the kids at recess. They were loud and raucous. There were groups playing tetherball and handball, some playing foursquare and chase. And then I saw Bailey. She was sitting alone under a tree. She was picking tiny white flowers and spinning them in her fingers. Kids raced by her, skipped by her, and no one stopped to call her name or even look her way. I pressed my hand to my mouth and felt hot tears rise in my eyes. Harrison walked up, took one look at my face, and said, "What's wrong?"

"She's totally alone again."

"What's she doing?"

I shook my head. "I don't know, but it's recess, and she's totally alone."

Harrison had grown up in a big house with a big family in the Vermont countryside where being alone was something to be treasured, but even he could see that there was something strange about how disconnected Bailey seemed from the life of the playground. "Maybe she's sick," he said, but when we spoke to her, she said she was feeling fine.

I don't even remember the play. As soon as I got home, I called a friend who was a therapist, got a number for a child psychologist, and made an appointment.

After listening to me for twenty minutes and Bailey for fifteen, the psychologist had the good sense to give Bailey some pens and paper and ask her to draw what she was feeling. Bailey drew a neon-orange city on the shore of a shocking-blue sea with a rainbow filling the sky. The sea had swirls of current. The city faded away from the shore as if she'd drawn it on a mathematically perfect grid. The rainbow was like an Escher strip, folding over itself like a ribbon of light. "I feel color," she explained.

"Tell me about that," the doctor suggested.

"I see color, I feel color, everything in the world for me is just color," Bailey said, as if she were stating something obvious and common to all ten-year-old girls. "Everything else gets in the way."

I was at that time a full-time staff photographer's assistant in the test kitchens at *Bon Appétit*. I looked for pattern and color and light in everything that was put in front of me, whether it was a bottle of Beaujolais, a barbecue-chicken pizza, or a glorious purple eggplant brought in that morning from the Central Valley. But what I realized when Bailey made her declaration to the psychologist is that looking in that way is my day job. It's something I elect to do, something I decide to do each day when I get up and go to work, and when I walk away from the camera, I leave it behind. Bailey couldn't walk away from the way she saw things. She lived with a heightened sensitivity toward the way things looked, like a dog who could hear a whole separate range of sounds. The world teemed with color to her, shouted with color; drawing—and later painting—was her effort to make sense of it all. She would always be the kind of person who scribbled in the margins.

I called Harrison to tell him about the relief Bailey felt at being understood, and the relief I felt at understanding, and then I called my dad to report the news—that Bailey was a natural, just like him. He had recently moved to Driggs in order to marry Caroline, the jewelry artist. He hadn't invited us to the wedding, and for retribution, I hadn't told him that I'd landed the position at *Bon Appétit*—or rather, I lied about what the job entailed. Instead of telling him that I was a food-photography intern, I told him I had a position in the test kitchens. He thought I did the dishes, minced the onions. The first time a photograph of mine appeared in the pages of the magazine—a two-by-three image of a mint-leaf sprig that was used to illustrate the table of contents—I bought a manila envelope so I could send it to him, but ended up throwing the whole thing into the garbage can at the post office, stamps and all.

But here was something he couldn't refute—a prodigy born of his own blood. He wasn't home when I called, so I left a message on his answering machine. "There's something exciting about Bailey I'd like to share with you," I said. "Call when you have a chance."

Two weeks went by with no phone call.

"He's communing with the fish," Harrison said. "He'll call when he comes in from the woods." Whenever we went to visit my dad, he and Harrison would disappear for days. They took noodles and carrots. They caught fish and fried them up in a little pan. When I asked Harrison what they talked about all that time—the Western mountain man and the son-in-law business guy—Harrison shrugged and said, "We don't talk with each other; we commune with the fish."

When two months went by with no response from my dad, I finally called again.

"Oh hey, Claire," he said. "How are things out there in California?"

"I left you a message about Bailey," I said.

"Did you?"

"A few months ago."

"Never got it," he said. "What is she, in third grade now?"

"Fourth. We took her to a psychologist for gifted kids."

"A shrink for kids? Jesus."

"Because she was drawing all the time."

"Nothing wrong with that," my dad said.

"No, I mean *all the time*. They think she's a kind of prodigy, a sort of savant." The sound of the words in my mouth tasted metallic, like blood. I was making an experience that had, in fact, been lovely sound like something steely and hard.

"Then you should send her out to visit," he said. "We'll be here in July. She doesn't have to go to school in July, does she?"

I jammed my teeth together, catching a tiny bit of the tip of my tongue between my front teeth, feeling a little pinch, holding my breath, willing myself not to say anything—not to say, *Who the fuck do you think you are?* Had he even sent Bailey a birthday present that year? Could he describe the color of her hair, if pressed? Had he forgotten what torture it had been when I came to visit around the same age?

"I'm building a cabin by a river," he said. "It's a huge thing. Huge beams, huge windows. It'll be finished in July and I'll buy her a huge bed. She can draw all day and all night if she wants." My dad laughed, then, a sick, self-satisfied guffaw. "It's funny," he said, "how something like that can skip a generation."

"How what?" I asked, because it was the thing that had gone unsaid between us my entire life and I suddenly wanted to hear him say it. Instead of living with the pain of pretending that it wasn't true, I could live with the pain of knowing that it was.

"How a genius for seeing can skip a generation just like blue eyes or a dimpled chin," he said.

His voice was smooth, polished. I had the distinct feeling that although I had never heard him speak those words, he had said them many times—to his lovers and wives, his friends and associates—but not to me, never to me. I felt something collapse inside me. It caved in, it crumbled, somewhere near my heart. At the same time I tasted the sharp tang of truth. It tasted like blood. I had the impulse to spit or vomit. "You really believe that?" I asked.

"They'll be able to prove that kind of thing one day," he said. "Mark my words."

I marked them, of course, though not in the way he meant.

*   *   *

Susannah, the art director, called to me down the hall-way, and I could tell from the sound of her voice that the news from New York wasn't good.

"Claire, these shots aren't working for us," she said.

I felt my stomach clench.

"They're falling a bit flat for us," she said.

"So what do we do?" I asked, because I had never actually let a client down before. I didn't know how it worked.

"Anita has authorized me to pay you a kill fee," she said. It was a fee written into every contract I'd ever signed. It was money paid when the client decided not to buy the shots they'd contracted for—a way for them to cut their losses. It was a horrible word. Kill fee. I pictured someone shooting a bullet through my photo-graphs. I saw the ragged hole, its singed edges. I could almost taste the acrid smoke.

She reached out a delicate hand and placed it on my shoulder. "I'm sorry," she said. "I know you've been going through a difficult personal time."

For a moment I thought that she knew, somehow, what had been going on in my head the last several days—the churning doubt, the cruel trick that made every image look somehow flawed. Then I realized that she was simply talking about my dad's death, and I managed to politely say, "Yes, thank you," though inside, I was cursing my dad, again, for choosing to die at such a particularly inopportune time.

CHAPTER FOUR

The first thing I did after having my story killed was to call my friend Bridget in Maine. Bridget had been in charge of graphic design at L.L.Bean for the last ten years. She cranked out catalogs with pictures of Bean boots and women in peacoats. She had no ambition to do anything other than what she was doing. She biked to work unless it was snowing. She ran through the woods on summer evenings, held the hockey-team banquet at her house each year. The most complicated food she ever encountered was a pot roast.

Ever since the day we met each other as college room-mates, Bridget has been like my own subconscious speaking out loud. After I helped my mother die, it was Bridget who suggested I sell the house where so much sadness had reigned. When my first marriage to a man I had met in school began to fizzle, it was Bridget who first uttered the words, *"What would happen if you were to leave him?"* No matter what the situation, she would say what had to be said.

"It's me," I said. "I totally screwed up a photo shoot."

"Screwed up, how?"

"I was shooting gorgeous artisan chocolate and jew-elry from Harry Winston and everything looked like crap—like cardboard crap—and they killed it."

"They killed it?" she whispered.

"Bang! Dead," I said, "And did I mention it was a feature for *Oprah*?"

"Oh my God."

"I know."

"But listen," she said—and this is precisely why I called, because Bridget would say "but listen" and then she would say something that made sense. "Every free-lancer screws up every now and then. Art directors know that."

"Yeah," I said, without an ounce of conviction.

"And your dad just died," Bridget went on. "People understand that it's a difficult time."

I shook my head even though she couldn't see. "I bet I'll never shoot for them again, and Harrison spent years courting this editor for me."

"Claire," she said, "it's not the end of the world."

"It was *Oprah*."

"It's not the end of the world. Do you know what you should do?"

I smiled at the possibility of a solution. "What should I do?"

"Go take a bath," she said, "and take some time to grieve for your dad."

I was still in the tub when Harrison came home—eyes closed, washcloth across my forehead, water hot enough to cook a lobster. I heard the garage door go up, heard Harrison's feet on the stairs, heard him unload his keys and phone and spare change in the closet. "Claire?" he called as he came through the door. "You in there?" I could hear the anticipation in his voice, the excitement at what he would find: his wife, naked and relaxed, perfumed by bubbles, eager to meet his lips with a tongue, his touch with a groan.

"Yeah," I said, "but don't get your hopes up."

"Hard day?" he asked.

"I screwed up the *Oprah* shoot."

"I'm sure you didn't..."

"No, I did," I said. "They killed it."

He scanned my face. "Are you serious?"

"Quite," I said.

"They can't just decide they don't want pictures of chocolate and jewelry—I mean, they can't just change their minds. You booked all your people, you took all that time. The kill fee is supposed to be for—"

"That's not what happened, Harrison. My photos sucked. They killed it because my photos sucked. It was like—I don't know," I said. "It was like I couldn't *see*."

He laughed. On the wall directly in front of me was a blown-up photograph I'd taken of a lemon. Just one lemon, with one green leaf still attached to it. It had been on the set of a barbecue shoot, and on a whim, I'd taken the lemon, propped it up with a toothpick in the sun, and snapped a picture. It looked like a globe, now, on my wall. Like a yellow planet. Like a whole, alien world.

"Why did your photos suck?" he asked quietly.

"I don't know," I said. "Everything just looked off to me, it just looked wrong. I couldn't get it right."

"You've never mentioned anything like this happening before," he said.

"That's because it never has."

"Is it something that's likely to happen again?" His question was totally practical. He didn't care about the crisis I experienced behind the lens, but about its impact on the business. He'd promised the *Oprah* editor that I wouldn't work for certain competing publications if they booked me, so we'd turned down work, let other clients go. He was selling me as if I were a commodity, which is exactly what I'd asked him to do—to make me into a marketable brand, to find me commercial success. But commodities didn't freak out over the tone of light. Commodities didn't take six hours to get one lousy shot of a block of gold bricks.

"I'm sure I'll be fine," I said. "I think I'm just exhausted. I'm going to take a few days to get on top of the stuff for the estate, and then I'll shoot the Limoncello billboards and I'll be fine when it's time for the Martha Stewart book."

"That's good," he said. "I'll call Susannah and see if there's anything I can do to appease her. And I'll call Michelle to assure her that everything's still a go for the cookbook."

"Thank you," I said. I lay back in the tub and imagined that the water was melting away whatever it was that had caused me to freeze up.

* * *

The next day, Bailey came into the kitchen, announced that she had finished her paintings, and promptly burst into tears.

"I still hate the seagull," she said, "but I have to be done. I just have to be done."

I reached out and folded her in my arms. "You've worked so hard," I said. "You should be so proud."

"I'm too tired to be proud."

"Why don't you go out to the beach? You haven't been out there all summer long. I'll take photos of the paintings while you relax."

"It would feel so good to lie in the sun."

"Then go. You deserve it."

I had Jim set up lights in Bailey's room, and went back with my Canon to take photos of the paintings, which would be used for the catalog and to send out to galleries and dealers. Bailey came back on her way to the beach, a bikini underneath her shorts and T-shirt. Her skin was pale from being inside so much, but it glistened with coconut oil. It smelled like summer. She was taller than I was, leaner, with eyes that were true blue and Harrison's patrician nose. When she was younger, she used to draw her hair with a crayon called Banana Mania and for mine she would use one called Dandelion, and that was exactly right; her hair was a more vibrant version of mine. When mine had recently become shot through with gray, it seemed as if that was the path it had been on all along when held up next to Bailey's.

"Thanks," she said, coming over to kiss me on the cheek. "Make them look good, will you?"

My work is all about setting the frame around a scene, arranging the light, looking for angles, looking for a point of view, and when I looked through the lens at Bailey's paintings, I could see that she had already done all that work. Her paintings had a wholeness to them, a weight, a purpose. Even the eye on the seagull looked flawless, perfect, exactly as joyful as she had hoped it would be.

When I set the seagull on the easel for its close-up, however, I saw a flaw. Through the powerful lens of my camera, I saw that there was a tiny hair stuck in the center of the bird's eye. A bristle from the paint-brush, an eyelash? I lowered the camera, approached the painting, and blew gently. When the piece of hair remained, I walked down the hall to my office, grabbed a can of compressed air, and tried to dislodge it with a more powerful blast. It didn't move. I picked up my camera again, thinking I would just ignore the hair, but it now appeared to me to be enormous, like a thorn.

I took the tiniest brush from the collection that was drying on a towel next to the sink. It was just a few hairs of a boar. I unscrewed the big tub of white paint that sat with all the other tubs on the steel baker's racks along the wall. I touched the brush to the pigment. I went up to the painting and set a tiny speck of white paint on top of the tiny hair to smooth it into place.

At that moment, Bailey walked in the door. Her hair hung wet to her shoulders. She had a towel knotted on her hips. "What are you doing?" she asked.

I reeled back from the canvas, the offending brush in my hand like a gun. "There was a piece of hair," I said, "in the eye."

She just stood there, gaping.

"I knew you'd want it to be perfect," I said.

"Perfect?" she hissed. "Who are you to judge what's perfect?"

She stormed toward a utility shelf that was crammed with carpet knives and bottles of glue, hammers, and a bucket of rags. She grabbed a can of spray paint, ripped off the cap, turned toward the soaring seagull. She sprayed a giant lime-green X across the middle of the painting, hurled down the can onto the cement floor, and bolted out the door,

CHAPTER FIVE

I *spent all* afternoon fielding phone calls. I approved the press release the museum wanted to send about their acquisition and repeated the same canned statement to a dozen reporters: *Our family is devastated by my father's death. We will do our best to carry out his wishes. I don't have a comment at this time on what those wishes are. We regret that we are not currently granting reprint permission for any images to be reproduced.*

Bailey came back that night while Harrison and I were eating dinner. She walked right by the table, said,

"Hey," grabbed an apple from the bowl on the counter, and headed straight upstairs to her room.

"She looks whipped," Harrison said.

I felt my face grow hot with shame. After she'd wielded the spray-paint can, I turned to go after her, then turned back and tried to wipe the paint off the canvas. There were individual splatters, tiny as pinheads, scattered like constellations all over the seagull. I grabbed a rag, wiped the mess. It was, perhaps, just thirty seconds since the paint had hit, but thirty seconds is a long time in the chemistry of paint. I tried turpentine, thought about nail polish. I ended up taking the painting and turning it against the wall.

"She's been working like a dog," I said, hoping to steer the conversation in a safe direction. "She definitely inherited your work ethic."

"I think about that all the time," he said. "How I was running Maple Hill Farms when I was her age. I had no idea what I was doing, but she seems so sure of herself. She blows me away."

"She's had the benefit of having a good dad," I said, and because of the smile on his face—a smile of utter satisfaction—I took the opportunity to ask how the deal was coming. He'd been staying up late at night staring at spreadsheets, running numbers. Vermont's annual Maple Festival was a few weeks away, and the principal investors from the group that was buying the business wanted to close the deal during the event in order to get maximum publicity.

"The closer it gets, the more I dread it," he said.

I reached across the table and took Harrison's hand in mine. He had long, elegant fingers I'd always thought were especially beautiful. "We can go back to the festival every year to relive the glory days," I said.

He grinned. We'd met the weekend of the Maple Syrup Festival in 1984. I was thirty-one years old, freshly divorced from a husband who was too much of a child to want children himself, and I was moonlighting, again, as a photographer at a friend's wedding because it was the only thing that brought me any joy. Harrison came up to me at the reception while I was taking a picture of the cake. He was tall and lean, with dark curly hair, brown eyes, and a seriousness of purpose that suggested that, although he may have spent his summers at yacht clubs and clambakes, his life wasn't all fun and games.

"It always seems a shame to eat the cake, doesn't it?" he said.

"I like cake," I said. "I think it would be a shame *not* to eat it."

"Cake's okay," he said, shrugging, "but I prefer pie myself."

"What kind of pie?" I asked, eyeing him.

"Excuse me?"

"What kind of pie do you like best?"

He smiled. "Blueberry, made right after picking, sweetened with maple syrup from the first tap."

I'd lived in New England long enough not to be fooled. First tap happened in the season when winter gave way to spring and blueberries ripened in August. "How do you get blueberries and maple syrup in the same season?"

"Through the miracle of modern food preservation," he said, and I laughed because I'd never met anyone who put their faith in such a thing, or dared to admit it.

"Modern food preservation?" I asked.

"Do I detect a hint of sarcasm?"

"No, I..."

"Without modern food preservation," he explained, "you would never have a prayer of this much butter-cream frosting, not to mention the grossly out-of-season crab cakes being passed around even as we speak. Are you a fan of maple syrup, by any chance?" he asked.

"I've been known to drown a waffle now and then."

He nodded. "That's good," he said. "Because I'm CEO of the largest family-owned maple-sugaring oper-ation in Vermont, and Tuesday is first tap. Come to Burlington and I'll make you a blueberry-and-maple-sugar pie."

"I'm not in the habit of driving four hours on the basis of a three-minute conversation and the promise of pie," I said. I had the urge to add, *Because I have to protect myself at every turn. I have to be vigilant. I have to keep up my guard.*

"I'm not either," he said, "but I would like it very much if you came."

He was pacing on the front porch when I arrived, and when I showed up, he whooped and ran out to my car to greet me. We trudged out to the trees with buckets, even though the gathering of sap in the traditional way was only ceremonial. The real business at hand was happening in vacuum tubes, under UV lights, with natural-gas evaporators, but who could ignore the thrill of tapping the trees under a crystal-clear early-spring sky the way people had done in those woods since the beginning of time? Kids whooped and ran through the trees, dogs ran in circles, long-married couples held hands, and Harrison narrated to me the history of his family farm. I felt myself drawn into his story, his voice, his smell. When he got to the part about the sap in the trees, he touched his finger to a tap and held a drop of the sweet liquid up to my lips. I had recently left a marriage in which sex had become burdened with expectation and disappointment, and where every kiss was fraught with meaning and peril and betrayal. I was hungry to be free of it. I darted my tongue out to taste the nectar and felt a flash of his skin on my tongue—rough and salty. I made a noise—something between "yum" and a tiny groan. He grabbed my hand and led me back through the woods to a barn that was stacked with old hay.

"Do that again," he whispered, and I didn't have any doubt what he meant or any doubt whether or not I wanted to comply. I took his hand, raised it to my mouth, and gently licked the end of his finger, and then he was kissing me furiously and I was kissing him back.

"I don't even live here," he said as he pulled my sweater over my head. "I live in Los Angeles."

His tongue tasted sweet, his hands were improbably warm. I pulled away from his kiss long enough to ask what the heir to a maple-sugar fortune was doing in L.A.

"I teach," he said, unzipping my boots. "I fly back here for board meetings. I flew back here for this."

"For this?" I asked, stepping out of my jeans.

"That's exactly right," he said.

When I called Harrison to tell him I was pregnant, he said, "Are you a fan of Los Angeles, by any chance?"

I'd never been to California, but I left the New England my dad had forsaken and my mom had cherished, and moved to the house on the sand.

"The glory days?" Harrison repeated. "What—you, me, and the bankers?"

I laughed. "I could bring my dad's attorney, too, and maybe the art director from the cupcake book."

"I'll be fine," Harrison said. "This deal will be done in ten days and then we have Bailey's exhibition, right? Seven P.M. on the fifteenth?"

At the mention of Bailey and the show, my whole body became taut. I could feel my forehead knit together, could feel my shoulders pinch. There would only be five paintings of the sea, not six. I wondered what her adviser would say. I wondered if there was a possibility Bailey might be denied her degree. "I think so," I said, and pretended as if suddenly there was nothing more important than standing up to clear the dishes.

I climbed into bed, curled into a ball, and tried to do what the yoga teachers call baby breathing, where you breathe through your nose and take the air all the way into your belly. It was supposed to be cleansing, nourishing, and grounding, but I often found that it just made me dizzy. And when I tried to remember Bailey asleep in her crib, I could never picture her breathing like that. I always had to lean down close to her body to see her little chest rise and fall and to get any sense at all that she was alive. Her breathing seemed so easy, so natural—nothing forced, nothing like mine. But I kept trying the baby breathing because I wanted so badly to believe that there was such a simple path to peace.

"You okay?" Harrison asked. He'd taken his clothes off, sat down on his side of the bed.

I shook my head. "No," I said softly, "I'm not."

He got under the covers beside me with his chest against my back, and wrapped his hands around me— one under my breasts across my belly, one resting on my hip. I felt his body begin to move and harden against me, and what I felt was the promise of oblivion. Sex, instead of talk. Sex, instead of thought. I arched back against him, inviting him to comfort me. He stroked my arms, my legs, my face. He combed his hands through my hair. When he cupped his hand between my legs, he did so in a way that made me feel as if I was fragile, cherished, and protected. It was exactly right. I pushed myself into his hand, and when he rolled on top of me, I arched to meet him.

Afterward, we lay together in the dark. The sound of the waves boomed through the room, and I could feel my heart try to slow and catch the rhythm. Lying there, feeling finally calm, I confessed to Harrison what I had done to Bailey's painting.

"Jesus, Claire," he said, sitting up and moving away. "What were you thinking?"

I searched my mind for an answer that made sense. I had been thinking about dust, I had been thinking about pieces of hair, I had been thinking about flecks of lint. I had been thinking about precision, perfection, the imperceptible difference between something that was ordinary and something that was so beautiful that it demanded attention. Maybe I had been remembering the time in third grade when Bailey was supposed to do five sheets of multiplication facts and had had a meltdown with half a page to go. Rather than letting her turn in an incomplete assignment, or writing a note to the teacher about the difficulty we were having, or helping her work through the stress of nine times seven, I did the math for her. I worked out the solutions, wrote down the answers on a piece of scratch paper, and told her to fill in the blanks. The paper came back that afternoon with *Nice job!* written in red ink across the top.

"I don't know what I was thinking," I said. "I swear it seemed so innocuous at the time. It seemed like I was just doing what I do all day, just making things look good, look better. It seemed like nothing."

"It wasn't nothing."

"Don't you think I know that by now, Harrison? She saw it happen. She walked in right when it happened."

"Oh my God."

"I know," I said. "And then she spray-painted a giant X across the painting. A lime-green X. It's totally ruined." I held my breath until he said something in response, and it seemed to take a very long time. I thought of tunnels, and of holding my breath. I thought of Princess Diana and how, if she still held her breath in tunnels, she would have died in the midst of a child-like challenge instead of just in an awful accident.

"Please say something," I finally said.

"I don't know what to say."

I threw back the covers on my side of the bed. "Maybe that you're sorry it happened?" I said. "Or, I don't know—'gee that sounds terrible, honey.'"

"It does sound terrible," he said. "For Bailey."

I stood up, threw on my robe. "So you're taking her side?" I asked. "Remember how she said she hated that bird? Maybe she was looking for a chance to ruin it."

"Could be," Harrison said. "But you definitely made a mistake. You definitely owe her an apology."

"I didn't ruin her painting," I said. I was beginning to feel frantic, desperate. I felt caged.

"You shouldn't have touched it at all," he said.

"I'm not an idiot, Harrison. I know I shouldn't have touched it. But I didn't ruin it."

He looked at me, his brown eyes hard as granite. "But did you want to?"

I stopped pacing and stared at him. "What kind of a mother do you think I am?" I asked. "You think I would deliberately ruin her painting because my father picked her over me? That would be beyond sick."

He stood, and tried to approach me. "You're a good mother, Claire," he said, "but this has been a tough time. There was the problem with the *Oprah* shoot, and I just thought that maybe you were . . . I don't know. Not in your right head. Overcome with grief."

"Well, the answer is no," I said. "I am not overcome with grief. You know how little I had to do with my dad. And I'm not out to sabotage you or Bailey or anyone else. I'm just trying to get through the day." I stormed out of the room and went downstairs to the studio to see if something had magically changed. Maybe fairies had come with pixie dust, or a genie with three wishes. I moved the painting out from the wall and spun it around. The green X was still there, awful and accusing.

There are so many times in the life of a mother when you orchestrate something—an outing or an outfit or a party—and you're convinced that your child will remember it forever. You think you're giving your kid a gift of a memory, wrapped up in a bow, but my experience has been that most of the time, the memory doesn't stick. It sticks in *your* head, but not theirs. I can remember, for example, when Harrison and I took Bailey to the Metropolitan Museum of Art in New York for the first time. It wasn't long after the meeting with the psychiatrist. We prepared by reading *From the Mixed-up Files of Mrs. Basil E. Frankweiler.* I got a hotel room at the Carlyle, just a few blocks away, so that we could walk to the museum, spend all day, then come back for high tea—a perfect New York day. When we climbed those wide front steps of the museum toward the fluted columns and big inner staircase, I swear I could hear violins playing. We took her to see Van Gogh's *Starry Night* in a special exhibit on the second floor. We got off the elevator, walked through one gallery of slightly lesser Impressionist paintings, turned a corner, and came face-to-face with that sky. "Look," Bailey said, pointing at the famous painting. "That looks just like the suns I draw." How could you forget a moment like that? It was seared into my memory. Yet Bailey forgot. She claims she never saw that painting on that visit. She claims she came upon it herself at MoMA one day her junior year in college, when she was trying to find a Seurat.

Somehow I knew, without even having to turn the matter over in my mind, that the green X wouldn't be like that. The green X would remain in our memories forever.

CHAPTER SIX

The *next morning,* I awoke early. It was still dark outside, and the wind was howling. I put on my robe, stepped into my felt slippers, and headed downstairs. From the kitchen I could see that the light was on in the studio. I walked across the flagstones beneath the whipping palm trees, went back to Bailey's studio, and knocked on the door. When she didn't answer, I knocked again, but still she didn't come. I stood there doing nothing for what seemed like a very long time, and then I turned the handle and cracked open the door.

She was wearing a "Heal the Bay" T-shirt and flannel pants and they were covered in paint. A slash of midnight blue ran from her elbow up toward her shoulder, as if she'd leaned against her painting, hugged it, danced with it. She had the earbuds in her ears, her iPod dropped into a flannel pocket at her hip. She had lately become obsessed with an art-rock band called Arcade Fire. They rehearsed and recorded their music in a nineteenth-century red-brick church in a small farm town outside Montreal. I could hear their distinct, rhythmic sound pulsing from her earplugs.

She stood at the easel, working on something new—a three-by-three-foot square. She had laid down paint on the background in great splotches of deep midnight blue; they bled into one another like stars colliding somewhere out in another galaxy. Arching across the middle of the canvas, she had pasted on a curved strip of something else—another piece of paper, painted with hot orange and neon green, that seemed fused onto the blue background.

I watched as she jammed a paintbrush at the palette, took a glob of silver paint, and moved in a kind of manic dance—turning, bopping, swinging as she washed the silver around the edges of the paper. Paint sprayed onto the cement floor, onto her pajama pants, onto the skin of her feet. She was reckless. She was brilliant. I felt, on the one hand, that I shouldn't watch, that what she was doing was private, intimate. But, on the other hand, I couldn't tear myself away. The air in the room was charged with something animal and alive. Bailey behaved as if she knew she couldn't make a wrong move. She couldn't pick the wrong color, couldn't put her brush in the wrong spot—and I wanted to be near that kind of faith, that kind of genius, if for no other reason than that I might figure out how it was done.

I finally erred on the side of caution. I stepped away.

Outside, the dried-out palm fronds were being ripped from the trees and flung to the ground, where they skid along like boats lost at sea. I walked around the side of the house and toward the beach. The second I stepped beyond the front patio, I felt the sting of sand on my skin. There was sand in my hair, sand in my eyes, and sand between my toes. I closed my mouth, squinted my eyes. The lights that lined the pier glowed through the chaos, awaiting sunrise. At the far northern end of the bay, I could make out the ghostly shape of the Santa Monica Mountains.

"What are you doing out here?" Harrison called from behind me. He'd opened and closed the patio door and the sound of the wind had completely concealed his movement. I could tell from the tone of his voice that he feared I had gone over the edge—wrecked a photo shoot, wrecked a painting, wandered out into a storm like a mad Shakespearean king.

"I'm looking at the sand," I shouted.

He raised his hand in front of his face, parted his fingers, peered out.

"The ridges," I said. The top layer of sand had been cut loose from the rest of the beach. It raced along, giddy with freedom. Beneath the frantic rush, small ripples had formed in a symmetry so perfect, it defied understanding. Stretching out from my feet, for as far as I could see, were ripples of the exact same width, between troughs of the exact same depth, as if no other shape were possible. "Don't you want to run out there and see how fast your footprints disappear?"

"No," he said. "I'm going back in. You coming?" His voice was concerned, pleading. He wanted to rein me in, get me back on track. I looked out at the water. Though the wind was commanding the sand into even ridges, it couldn't control the sea. The water was all frothy chaos. Enormous waves rose and crashed to shore as if they were being hurled by an angry god. I shook my head no.

I took off my shoes and stepped onto the sand. There was not one other person in sight—not one runner, not one lifeguard, not anyone leaning their body into the wind as they made their way along the beach. I leaped forward, disrupting five perfect ridges. My feet sank into the sand as they always do—deep scoop of heel, shallow scoop of toes—but the moment I shifted and moved forward, sand raced to fill the hollow I'd left behind, to smooth it over, to make it obey the wish of the wind.

I ran into the storm with my head down, my eyes squinted shut. I let my body fall into the wind, and here's the miraculous thing: it held me.

On my way back to the house, I saw one other person: my neighbor, the old opera singer, Mrs. Jenkins. She was standing at her living-room window, looking out at the angry clouds over the water. When I looked in her direction, she waved me over.

I stepped onto her patio and stood right up next to the glass. "Good morning," I yelled.

"Looks like fun," she said. Her words sounded muted and muffled through the glass and the wind. She was twelve years older than my father would have been, and she still lived alone, still dressed herself every day, still walked to the pier and back, slowly, when the temperature was right. She had been a mezzo-soprano. She had been a star. She once played me the recording of her debut, which she made at the age of twenty-seven, singing *Carmen* at the Met. She sat and listened with me, concentrating on each note as if it were still her job to produce sound like that.

"Come out and join me," I said.

She shook her head and smiled wistfully. "Too old for that."

"I'll hold you up. The wind will hold you up."

She shook her head again. "I'll enjoy it from here."

I waved good-bye and stepped off her patio, back into the stronger wind. "Wheeeeee," I called, for her benefit, and spun in a circle that sent my hair flying. From behind the safety of the glass, she was laughing.

When I came back inside, Harrison was in the kitchen making coffee. "Did you talk to Bailey?" he asked.

"She's in the studio," I said. "I don't think she slept last night. I mean, I don't think she went to sleep at all. I think she's painting something new."

"So did you talk to her?"

"Not yet," I said. I had rehearsed apologies in my head all morning—*I'm sorry, it was so wrong, I didn't do it out of jealousy, I swear*—but they all sounded disingenuous.

Harrison had poured milk into a small pitcher, poured Rice Krispies into a bowl, and put them on an orange melamine tray, which he was taking out to the studio. I stared after him as he made his way through the wind. I live in a world where food is far more than mere sustenance. To the people who take pictures of food, write about food, or cook food that will be talked about at dinner parties and discussed over chopping blocks all over the country, food is a sensuous pleasure, but it's also a precious commodity—a way of stating your status, of keeping your place in society. I remember going to a Cinco de Mayo party not long after I was hired full-time at *Bon Appétit*. The hosts, two celebrity chefs who had recently landed a TV show, made their own tortillas in a twenty-year-old cast-iron skillet, chopped the homegrown tomatoes and jalapeño peppers with a $150 knife, mashed the avocados in a marble mortar and pestle that, they said, had once been used by a Balinese medicine man, and served tender chicken mole that had been simmering for two days in chocolate they'd personally carried back from Barcelona. We, the guests, were delighted and awed. That was our job, to be impressed, and we left buzzing about the couple's taste, their generosity, and how we were looking forward to working with people who paid such passionate attention to the minutiae of food.

But if you want to make a simple statement—to tell someone you love them or that you're sorry—it's often the simplest, most unpretentious foods that do the trick. Tea and toast. Chicken-noodle soup. Chocolate-chip cookies. A bowl of Rice Krispies. I grew up in New England with a mother who was a master of these foods. She comforted the whole town with her chicken-noodle soup, until she was the one who needed comfort herself. I came directly home from college to take care of her, which meant that I took over the cooking. I chopped the celery to make the chicken stock that we believed might cure her, shelled the walnuts to make cookies for people who came to visit, and figured out how to brew the perfect cup of chamomile tea with honey—which in the end was all she could stomach. As I watched Harrison from the kitchen table, his cereal offering struck me as one of the nicest things I'd ever seen anyone do, and as much as I loved him for it—he was such a good father, such a caring man—I wished I'd thought of it first.

Bailey stayed in her studio all day. At 6 P.M., Harrison made her a turkey sandwich. When he came back from delivering it, I was in the bedroom getting ready for a party I didn't want to go to.

"She's doing something new," he said.

"I saw it," I said. "A new painting."

"No, it's a totally new technique," he said. "She's

cutting and slicing things, building up layers. There's paper all over the place. It's pretty amazing."

I thought suddenly of the strip of neon green I'd seen on her canvas that morning. "Did she cut up the seagull?"

"She did," Harrison said.

"She must be so furious with me," I said quietly.

Harrison pulled a Tommy Bahama silk shirt off a hanger, slipped it on, didn't say a word.

"And you, too? You still think I did it on purpose?"

He looked up. "I don't want to think that," he said.

Bailey was still out in the studio when we came home at eleven thirty.

"I'm going out there to tell her to stop," I said. "She's going to make herself sick."

"She's twenty-three years old," he said. "I don't think you can tell her to do anything."

"Okay," I said. "Then I'm going to apologize."

I walked out to the studio and stood, once again, at the door. She was asleep on the couch in her clothes, with all the lights blazing. The new painting was on the easel. It was a collage, made up of layers of painted paper—some of them strips that had been sliced out of the ruined seagull painting. I saw a strip of the hot-pink sky. I saw three strips of lime-green spray-paint-flecked saffron-colored wings. Woven in were bits of paper with a silver metallic thread, which thrust up off the surface of the painting like splashes of water. The painting depicted a wave that rose from the top right corner in riotous layers of colors, and broke in a froth on the lower left. The spray from the wave burst beyond the edge of the canvas. Green and blue flecks of roiled water seemed to hang in midair, suspended in time. It looked exactly as if the wave had just broken, as if the viewer might have to shield her face. Harrison had been right: this was something entirely new—more energetic, more confident, more technically advanced than anything she'd ever done. And it was decidedly amazing.

I turned out the lights and went to bed.

Bailey came up to me the next morning while I was making coffee and stood on the far side of the kitchen island. She had circles under her eyes—actual purple half-moons.

"Can I borrow your camera?" she asked. "I need a shot of a new painting."

"Bailey, I'd be happy to—"

"I just want to know if I can borrow your camera."

I looked away from her, toward the ocean, where the sun was shining as if there hadn't been such a fury yesterday, as if nothing had ever been wrong. "It's in the studio," I said. "In the top drawer of my desk."

She turned to go.

"Do you know how to download the shots?" I called after her.

Without looking back, she said, "I'm sure I can figure it out."

While Bailey took my camera into her studio, I stepped outside onto the patio. I sat on one of the teak chaises and watched a leaf spin down from the sky and a hummingbird feeding at the lavender that grew in enormous terra-cotta pots along the fence, and then got out my cell phone and called Bridget.

"I did something terrible," I said.

"Again?"

"I did something to one of Bailey's paintings and she got mad and she wrecked it."

"What do you mean, she wrecked it?"

"She sprayed a lime-green X across the middle."

"What did you do to warrant *that*?"

"There was this piece of hair. I painted over it."

"You *painted* on Bailey's painting?"

"I know," I said, and felt my whole face screw up as I started to cry. "I told you it was bad."

"You weren't kidding."

"You're supposed to make me feel better," I said. "You're doing a lousy job."

"Okay," she said. "Why don't you go back and tell me what the hell you were thinking. I mean, why'd you do it?"

"I don't know," I said. "I don't know."

"What I don't get is that you're the mom who wouldn't even put ketchup on Bailey's hamburger because she had a special way of swirling it around the bun, and this was a painting for her MFA show. Are you worried about her? I mean about the paintings being good enough?"

"Bridget, it was a tiny hair. A teeny, tiny hair. It's not like I decided to change the shape of the bird's beak."

"So it wasn't that you wanted to make the painting somehow better?"

"No," I said. "No one could do anything to make Bailey's paintings better. They're amazing. You should see them. They have this presence to them, this magic. They're amazing."

Neither of us said anything for a moment, and then Bridget said softly, "Could you be jealous, Claire?"

My heart began to pound as if I'd been caught. Jealous of my own daughter? Jealous of her talent, of her easy relationship with my dad, of the fact that she had never lived a day doubting that her art was worth doing? Of course I was jealous. Who wouldn't be? But that's not what was driving me when I stood in front of her canvas with the little boar brush, and I would have sworn it to a jury. "No," I said softly, "that's not it. It was something else. Something happened when I was in front of the painting that was like a weird trick of the eye. The hair looked enormous. Like a thorn. I couldn't see anything but that hair."

"Are you talking about an ophthalmological problem?" Bridget asked.

"You're asking me if I need *glasses*?"

"I thought bad eyesight was a reasonable possibility."

"No," I said. "The same thing happened on the chocolate shoot. Everything just looked somehow *off*. It's like something got switched off in my brain, some connection. It's like something snapped. I don't know what's going on."

Neither of us said anything for a moment. The air crackled between us, waiting to be filled with conversation. I was about to say, *Are you still there?* when

Bridget finally said, "Your dad just died. This isn't a big mystery."

I closed my eyes. The news had gotten out that my dad had destroyed a huge number of negatives before he took his little outing up to the top of Fred's Mountain and that the only person who had the right to make any additional prints from the remaining negatives was Bailey. The value of his existing work had increased exponentially in value. It was the talk of the art world. He would have been so pleased.

"What does my dad's dying have to do with anything?" I asked. "Maybe it's just that...I don't know. Maybe I've just lost my touch."

"You're a GK," Bridget said, in a voice that didn't seem at all friendly, "and GKs don't suddenly lose their touch the moment the man dies."

"What on earth is a GK?"

"Genius's kid. Like priest's kid, only usually a lot wealthier. Didn't you see that *Rolling Stones* cover story on the kids of rock stars? Art Garfunkel has a son who plays the guitar and John Lennon's kid can apparently really sing. Can you imagine being John Lennon's kid and deciding that you were going to open your mouth to sing?"

"I missed that issue," I said coldly, "but I'm not a

genius kid, because in case you forgot this part of my history, I barely lived with my father."

"It's something you may want to think about," she said.

"Thanks," I said. "This has been very illuminating."

"Anytime," she said.

CHAPTER SEVEN

*G*enius *was the* excuse my mother always made for my father. Until the Vietnam War started, my dad ran an engineering firm in Maine. He built bridges and buildings, and consulted with towns on their infrastructure budgets. Soon after Kennedy was shot, however, when the idea of a draft came up, he immediately volunteered for active duty. He'd gone through college on an ROTC scholarship, and he felt that it was his duty to set an example for the younger men who were balking about serving their country. It was 1964, a year before students marched on Washington to protest the war. He went to Danang and took photos that the Army Corps of Engineers needed for their mapmaking efforts, and, in the midst of those green hills and that humid heat, decided that he'd missed his calling. His tour of duty in Vietnam made him pine to take photos of an America he'd never seen—the open-road America of Jack Kerouac, the soulful free America of Bob Dylan.

He came home, and started packing to leave again. He told me not to worry because ours was a great country and he would be back soon. He told my mom she was doing a great job holding down the fort and that she should keep up the good work. He told our neighbor that his plan was to head to the great mountain ranges of the West and start taking pictures the way Edward Weston, the brilliant philandering cohort of Ansel Adams, did—with passion, with an unshakable belief in the sanctity of the moment. All this should have set off alarms, but there were so many alarms going off in the country at that time that it was hard to figure out what any one of them might mean. He took off in our pale yellow station wagon, and after that all we got were postcards.

It's hot, he would write in Santa Fe, *but the light is good at sunrise.* Or from Boise, he'd say, *Staying on a ranch in the shadow of the Sawtooth Range, eating beans for breakfast.*

"Beans for breakfast?" I asked my mom as I sat in front of my oatmeal. "That's disgusting."

While my mother was left to serve as a secretary to engineers who were not her husband, my dad wandered around meeting cowboys who drove herd at tree line, ranchers who had never been out of sight of the peaks that stood guard over their plot of land, and women who knew exactly how to love a man who loved a mountain. And somehow, for him, something magical happened in the mix of what he was doing. Somehow he did exactly what he set out to do, which had nothing, unfortunately, to do with us.

Not realizing that unschooled neophytes don't just send photos to the home of Albert Eisenstadt and Herb Ritts, my dad sent a batch of prints to *Life* magazine. He liked to say that he just wrote *Art Director* on the envelope and popped it in the mail, but who knows, at this point, what is true and what is tall tale. In any case, the art director wrote him back and offered to buy a photograph of Mount Whitney at sunset and he asked to see anything else my dad might want to send along.

The next envelope my dad sent included a piece

of yellow legal-pad paper with the words *The Secrets of American Mountains* scrawled on it with a pencil borrowed from the fry cook at the Lamb's Grill Café in Salt Lake City, Utah. Among those shots was a series of the Sawtooth Range in all four seasons—its aspen trees in fall color, the starkness of its jagged, rocky peaks covered in snow. The art director bought the whole series, and asked, again, for more.

Before too long, the Field Museum in Chicago called to offer my dad a fat commission to continue what he was doing. The result was a mail-order divorce from my mother and a book of photographs called *The Secrets of American Mountains*. The book led to an appointment at the University of Washington to teach photography, a gig as a guest columnist at *Popular Photography* magazine, and solo shows in galleries from Sun Valley to Santa Fe. My dad became an expert, a sage, someone who had something important to say about America in the twentieth century. Journalists called to ask him about the future of open spaces. The Sierra Club and Earth First! invited him for their conferences. He kept taking his photos, and giving his opinions, and in 1978, the MacArthur Foundation called.

He'd won a genius award.

My mother had been right all along.

* * *

The summer after the Summer of Love, my dad invited me to come out and travel with him for two weeks of my vacation. It was during his Field Museum commission but before the MacArthur call. I was fifteen years old and hadn't spent more than a few days with him since the time he'd left three years before. I had adopted a righteous hatred of all the adults around me who were sending my friends' older brothers to be gunned down in rice paddies halfway around the world and who were still listening to Tommy Dorsey when you could listen to the Beatles. And because my dad had actually walked away from all that, because he was actually living a life of pure freedom and romance, I hated him most of all.

"But of course you'll go!" my mother cried.

What would cause a woman to still love a man who'd left her for a camera? My mother treasured the postcards my dad sent. She bought twenty copies of the first *National Geographic* issue that featured his photos and handed them out to all her friends and neighbors. A print of his image of twilight in the Rockies hung in the place of honor over her fireplace until the day she died. And every year on his birthday, whether he was living with another woman or not, my mom would bake him a batch of her Scottish mother's shortbread and send it to him packed tightly in a tin with best wishes for a happy year. The fact was that my mom never stopped loving my dad.

I said yes—I'd go visit—because she would never be invited.

"Just make sure you read Abbey before you come," my dad instructed, "and bring a hat."

"Who's Abbey?" I asked.

"Edward Abbey," he said. "A writer."

The clerk at Sherman's Bookstore in Bar Harbor, Maine, had never heard of him, so I went to the library and asked the librarian if she could help me.

She thumbed through a stack of *Reader's Digest* magazines, pulled one out, and showed me an article by Edward Abbey, a writer who had spent a season as a ranger in Arches National Park.

"It's a desert out there," the librarian explained to me. "Very sparse and dry." Our local national park—Acadia—was lush, green, and ocean-bound, a place for rocky beaches, pine trees, and black bears.

I requested a copy of Abbey's *Desert Solitaire*, and picked it up three weeks later. I had, up until that time, mostly read Nancy Drew mysteries and thick novels about the English aristocracy. Edward Abbey was a revelation. I took to hiding the book under my pillow, not only because I didn't want my mother to know that I was taking direction from my dad, but because on page 86 was the word *fuck*. On page 123, there was a rant against vacationers who sped through the national parks with a checklist that sounded exactly like every family from Maine I had ever met. But the real reason that Abbey was dangerous was that he explained, clearly and unflinchingly, who my dad was. Not Huck Finn, after all. Not even Edward Weston. My dad was actually Edward Abbey. The West was his religion. The land was his temple. He hadn't run away when he left me and my mother; he had run home.

Understanding my dad did little to help me like him. My ten days in and around Moab, Utah, were uncomfortable for a dozen different reasons. Abbey had made the place seem like a cathedral, but it was hard to appreciate the colors and patterns and light because it was so unrelentingly hot. I was hot when I woke up, hot all day, hot in the middle of the night. The heat seemed fused to me like a second skin. I also disliked sleeping on the ground, where I knew for a fact there were snakes and lizards and red ants, because I had seen them scurrying about. Their presence didn't make me feel close to the earth; it made me nervous. It might have been better had my dad talked to me. He could have asked me about Mom or school or what I thought of the red rock. He could have taught me about f-stops or filters or zoom lenses, but I would have to figure out those things on my own. My dad wasn't interested in conversation, and he wasn't interested in me. I was there, I realized, simply to bear witness to his genius—and, I would soon learn, to be tested.

When he picked me up in Salt Lake, he handed me a camera. It was the first thirty-five-millimeter camera I ever held—a Nikon F, with a black steel case with a leatherette finish. It was heavy, and I felt its power and its fragility the moment I picked it up. "Thought you might like to give it a whirl," he said. "You've got twenty-four shots there. Let's see what you can do."

My dad could spend five days waiting for inspiration to strike. We would drive in his Jeep to a trailhead, then climb all day to get to a certain plateau, tramp around for two hours checking out the views, then choose a rock and lie on it, sit on it, stand on it awhile, then choose another rock until finally he deemed it the place to set up his tripod and camera. I trailed after him trying to see what he saw. I looked out across the vast dry landscape at the La Salle Mountains in the distance, but all I could see was the same thing you could see from the point a half mile to the south where we had been an hour before. He seemed not to be taking many photos in each of the places where he set up. He would crouch under the black fabric, peer through the lens, insert the thick glass plates, but I didn't often hear the sound of his camera clicking—a sound I loved. It sounded exactly like a cricket gearing up to chirp through the night—a deep, many-layered whir. I couldn't figure out how he knew when to press the shutter and when to leave it be. It seemed like he operated by some unseen set of rules, some otherworldly guide.

I pointed my Nikon at the sunset and pressed the release. I pointed it at juniper trees and boulders, at three fire ants carrying a beetle, at a water bug skimming the surface of a green, gunked-up pool of rainwater. Before he'd taken one shot, I'd taken all twenty-four of mine.

We developed the film in the little darkroom he had set up in one of the bathrooms of the house he was renting by the river—or rather, *he* developed them. I stood and watched as he mixed the chemicals and dropped the negatives one at a time into the sink. I held my breath as the images emerged, expecting to see exactly what I'd seen standing on the mesa: sunset, trees, rocks, insects. All that was visible, however, were splotches of light and dark, fuzzy outlines of things that could have been rocks but could just as easily have been stacks of hay. I looked at him, expecting him to explain what I had done wrong, or what could be done right, but all he said was, "You can try again tomorrow." I was supposed to divine how to filter light, how to set film speed, how to gauge the depth of field, and the next day, I tried again.

While my dad set up his tripod, fussed with his film, and pointed his lens at the far horizon, I spent half an hour circling a juniper tree looking for branches that might reveal something mysterious, and sage-green berries that might speak deep truths, and then I spent the next half hour trying to remember how things had been set the day before and trying to figure out what each dial on the Nikon might do to make the outcome better. I was desperate not to make a mistake, not to get things wrong again. Out of a roll of film with twenty exposures, I painstakingly eked out three shots.

We headed back to the Jeep in darkness, through the scrub and the rock. There was no trail. There was barely any light. Before we made it to the car, I tripped and fell, and the camera flew from my hands and landed with a terrible crack. I ignored my throbbing knees and stood to recover the camera. When I lifted it from the ground, I saw that the glass lens was shattered.

"Goddamn it, Claire!" my dad bellowed. It seemed to me that the words came out of his mouth before the camera even hit the ground, before the crunch of lens on rock betrayed what had happened, before my knees became bloody and my hands scraped raw.

When we got in the car, I looked out into the vast blackness, and after a while, I asked if the camera would be okay.

"Nope," he said.

"But we'll be able to develop the pictures, won't we?"

"Nope," he said.

I felt crushed, defeated. I'd worked so hard. "I didn't know how hard it was to be a photographer," I said.

He laughed in a way that meant he wasn't amused. "Girls don't have to worry about being anything," he said, conveniently choosing to ignore the fact that his leaving us had meant that my mom had to worry about being everything. I didn't know, then, about Imogen Cunningham, whose portraits of plants and people were exhibited alongside works by Ansel Adams and Edward Weston in the 1930s. I didn't know about Diane Arbus, who became famous taking riveting photos of society's fringe. I couldn't imagine Annie Leibovitz, who would become as much of a celebrity as the celebrities whose photos she took. All I knew was that my dad, Paul Switzer, the famous photographer of the American West, didn't think that a girl—or at least *his* girl—could be a photographer.

He gave me a sketchbook to use for the remainder of my time in Moab. When I brought it home, my mother commented on how nice that was of him to encourage my drawing—an activity I had no interest in or aptitude for—and when he invited me to visit him out west again, she urged me to go because he was my father, after all, and nothing could replace family. I spent a week in Ketchum, Idaho, when I was seventeen, and a week in Jackson Hole just before I went off to college, but each time, I brought romantic novels to read—*Love Story* and *The Winds of War.*

It was ten years before I touched a camera again.

CHAPTER EIGHT

I had to fly back to Driggs to meet with the curator from the Center for Creative Photography. His name was Alex Kepler—like the astronomer, he said—and although he'd expressed all the proper condolences to me—*I'm sorry for your loss; your father was an inspiration to generations of photographers; these photos will add immeasurably to the museum's collection*—I could tell that he was in a hurry to locate the images that were his, crate them up, and get them safely back to

Phoenix. The ice in the Teton River was still frozen solid, but Alex Kepler was eager to get to work.

"Bailey won't be able to join us," I'd told him over the phone. I said something about the fact that she was in the final stages of preparation for her thesis exhibition, but that was a lie. All she had left to do was to write an artist's statement and choose an outfit to wear. The truth was that she couldn't stand to be alone in a room with me, let alone a ten-seat plane bouncing through the mountains out of Salt Lake. Her paintings were done, her show would open in a week, and I expected that once it was over she would pack up her duffel bags, move back to her stifling little apartment in Pasadena with her sculptor roommate, and start applying to teach somewhere—all without saying a word to me.

I had arranged to meet Alex at the general store, and when I walked in, I picked him out immediately. He was wearing a coat and tie and a pair of polished loafers that would last about two minutes in the frozen slush. His hair was the color of carrots.

"Claire," he said, when I approached the table. He

stood to pump my hand and towered over me—an orange-toned, bespectacled Ichabod Crane. "It's such a pleasure to meet you."

"Did you find it okay?" I asked, sweeping my hand to take in the old linoleum floor, the soda fountain, the spinning rack of postcards.

"No problem," he said. "Your directions were spot on."

"It's much harder to find the house," I said. "Would you like coffee, or shall we head over?"

"Let's go before we lose the light," he said, and before he'd even finished the sentence, he'd turned and snatched up his coat and his gloves.

I led him out Route 33, turned onto the second unmarked road on the right, and followed the frozen river until it took a turn to the left. My dad's driveway peeled off to the right a quarter mile later. We went first to the guesthouse over the garage, where Alex would be staying while he did his work. He'd have a million-dollar view of the mountains, a woodburning stove, a galley kitchen stocked with cans of soup, boxes of noo-dles, and jars of tomato sauce. I showed him where the firewood was kept and how to light the stove, and then walked him over to the main house.

"Spectacular," he pronounced, when we stepped through the front door. He stood in the foyer and took in the massive beams, the soaring ceilings, the picture windows that framed the mountains, which were reflecting the last bit of the day's sun. It took most people a few minutes to recognize the art, but before he even took a step beyond the entry, Alex had identified the three Remington sculptures mounted in the foyer, the Edward Weston nude over the fireplace, the Eliot Porter pond reflection in the hallway. He approached a collection of fishing lures mounted in a frame in a bookcase, and read their names—*elk-haired caddis, parachute adams, serendipity*. "I can feel his spirit here," he said, as if he thought these were exactly the words I wanted to hear.

I took a deep breath and tried not to say anything snide. I was twenty-two years old when my mother died, and I had counted on feeling her spirit. She hadn't gotten a very good deal out of life—divorce at a time and place when everyone else stayed married; hard work in a field she didn't choose; an early death from a cancer she couldn't control—and I counted on the fact that it would all be made up to her in death. I imagined that her spirit was on a romp through heaven, and that she would join me when I went to church and sang the soaring Protestant hymns I had learned at her side or when I made an apple pie from honeycrisp apples, which were her favorite. I went to bed each night certain that she would come to me in a dream and tell me how great everything was, now that she wasn't sick and alone. But dead, it turned out, was just dead, so when my dad died, I had no expectations whatsoever about his spirit and was even less interested in trying to conjure it up.

I forced a smile. "Let me show you the study," I said.

I led him down the hall to the big room behind the garage. Along two walls were custom-made floor-to-ceiling bookcases crammed with biographies and histories, books of photography, and boxes of negatives, transparencies, and prints. In front of the west wall were flat files, letter files, and a curtained door that led to a small vestibule that led to the darkroom, where the cameras in their cases were stored in blackness and silence. The fourth wall was faced in cork, and pinned with a blizzard of images, newspaper clippings, magazine advertisements, greeting cards, invitations, citations. The center of the study was dominated by a large wooden island, stool height, with two large built-in light boxes. The viewfinders were still where my dad had left them, the pens, the Post-it notes, the old-fashioned Rolodexes, the bottle of Mccallan, the river-rock paperweights, the paper clips.

"His sense of organization came and went," I said, "in direct proportion to the organizational interests of the women who came and went. There were some years when he tossed everything in cardboard boxes and others when he had fawning interns who obsessed over every last transparency. I'm awfully glad I'm not the one who has to catalog it."

"Don't worry about that," Alex said, setting his laptop on the central wooden table. "I'll begin the work and the museum will send an archivist to take care of everything else." He fussed with the computer for a moment, opening it up, switching it on. "I'll need to speak with Bailey as soon as possible," he said, "to see what she has in mind for the retrospective. I don't want to get too far out in front of her."

What she has in mind for the show, I thought, *is precisely nothing. She's consumed with her own work and furious with me. But this is what my esteemed father so desperately wanted, so this is what you're going to get.*

I nodded. "I understand," I said. "At the moment she's preparing for her MFA exhibition. It's next week, actually. She's quite concerned about what to wear." I laughed nervously, because what to wear had been a question that was weighing heavily on my mind. Was I, in fact, still invited to the show? Would I dare show up? And if so, what did a mother wear who was proud and contrite, jealous and thrilled, amazed and full of doubt?

"That's an exciting time," Alex said. "I've watched a

lot of people go through it. Eat, sleep, paint. It can be intense."

He pushed some buttons on his keyboard, brought up some documents. "You know your father and I corresponded before his death," Alex said.

I nodded again. "It was a busy time for him," I said, wondering if he would hear the irony in my voice and take the bait—but he didn't.

"He said that *American Buffalo* is on loan at the Wildlife Museum?"

"It's over in Jackson."

"I'll be contacting the curator over there," Alex went on. "And he mentioned that a doctor friend has *Morning Trout* hanging in his home?"

"That's Sam next door," I said, pointing north. "That will be no problem. My dad gave Sam many gifts over the years, but that one was on loan. He knows it's not his."

"Good," Alex said, "I'd like to take all the remaining negatives back to Phoenix when I go, if that's okay."

I shrugged. Bailey was the only one who could authorize any additional prints, but the center would want to protect their new acquisition; it made sense for him to take them away.

"The will stipulates that we hang the retrospective within a calendar year of his death, so we'll need to work fast to decide on collateral publications, posters, publicity."

"I'll let her know," I said, deciding, suddenly, that I didn't really like Alex Kepler and wanted him gone as fast as he seemed to want to go.

"Can I work late here in the house?" Alex asked. "I don't want to bother you, or invade your privacy; it's just that as long as I'm here, I might as well work."

"That's fine," I said. "Just let yourself out the front door when you're done."

I made myself a burrito in my dad's polished granite kitchen, and then went down the hallway to Bailey's room. My dad had come through with his promise, and bought her an enormous bed. It was a California king. The headboard, footboard, and canopy frame were made of rough-hewn split pine. Curtains of heavy green velvet with a burnout pattern of pine needles hung around the entire bed. You could turn off the lights, close the curtains, and see nothing but starlight shining through the slivers in the fabric. It was like being in the forest at night—but a warm, comfortable, down-filled forest. Bailey used to leave our house on the sand and come up here every summer; I would fly her out, stay a night in a lesser guest room, and then leave her to sleep in that magical bed and wander the woods with my dad. They sketched the cows in the fields by the road, took pictures on the top of peaks they climbed, had the town's famous huckleberry milk shakes for breakfast, lunch, and dinner.

I had hoped that Bailey could be a bridge between us—a reason for détente. But I used to sit home in L.A. while she was gone and count the hours until I could go and retrieve her. And then, when she was back in my presence, I sat miserably and listened to her go on and on about how wonderful he was, how understanding, how patient, how good, how wise, and I would grit my teeth and say, *How nice.* Once, when I came to pick up Bailey after a four-week visit, I found her and my dad out back by the river. It was a sparkling clear day, and they were sitting on the lawn painting with watercolors. They had paper clipped onto wooden boards, little cakes of paint. They didn't raise their heads when I appeared. "Paper's wet, can't stop," Bailey said, so I went back to the car, brought in my carry-on, had a glass of water in the kitchen. When I went back outside, they were still painting. I stood over them and saw an image of the river on each of their pieces of paper—rocks, reeds, water, a flash of fish. I stood there, completely outside of their circle, wondering what they were doing, why it demanded silence. After a while, Bailey said, "My paper's dry."

"So I win," my dad said.

"No you don't," Bailey argued. "I have all the elements."

"Let me see that." My dad snatched Bailey's board, and scanned her paper. I had no idea what he was looking for. "You did it!" he said.

"Of course I did," she said. She grabbed his board and looked over what he had done. Again, I tried to figure out their game. "You, too?" she asked.

"Damn straight," he said.

"No winner, then," she said.

"My composition is better."

"My execution is better."

"Isn't anyone going to say hello?" I asked.

They looked up at me. "Hi, Mom," Bailey said.

"Lend us your opinion, Claire. Wet paper, a dry brush, three colors. The challenge was to include every color in the rainbow in a river scene. Who won?"

I looked at the paintings. They were both beautiful. I shrugged. "Seems to me you both did," I said, but it was clear from their blank looks that I had said the wrong thing.

* * *

It was on one of her trips to Driggs that Bailey told my dad the truth about what I did at *Bon Appétit*. She showed him a spread that featured a photo I'd taken of a chocolate layer cake. I always imagined that she was bursting with pride when she brought it out of her suitcase. A child of twelve couldn't possibly discern the difference in value between a panoramic photograph of a mountain and a magazine spread of party food. She was surely proud. I also imagine that he said something kind to her about me—something sympathetic or at least benign. But he sent it back to me in a large envelope. A three-by-five card was paper-clipped to the photo, with these words scrawled in response to the revelation that I, too, was a photographer: *Nice light on the left, too much light on the right.*

I'd never actually slept in Bailey's bed before. I set my duffel bag on the window seat, then closed the curtains around the bed and walked around the outside, examining it. I changed into my pajamas—flannel, plaid, men's cut—and turned off the light and crawled inside. I sat there awhile, letting my eyes adjust, and then I reached for my cell phone, lay back on the pillows, and called Bailey.

"It's Mom," I said, when she answered.

"I know. Caller ID," she said.

"So you still picked up?" I asked.

She took a breath, let it out. "What are you calling about?" she asked.

"I met the curator today. Alex Kepler. He's going to want you to come out and talk things over."

"I told you I would go after my exhibition."

"I know. I just thought ... I mean, is there anything you want me to tell him now, while he's getting started? He seems kind of eager."

"What would I want to tell him?"

"I don't know, Bailey, I'm just trying to be helpful."

"Because you've been so helpful with *my* work?"

"That's not fair," I said quietly.

"Not fair?" she shot back.

She wanted to fight, but I didn't need to; I knew I had already lost the battle. "Bailey, I'm sorry about what I did to your painting," I said.

"I'm sure you are," she said.

"What's that supposed to mean?"

"Just that sorry is the easy response. You hurt someone's feelings and you say you're sorry. You hit someone with your car and you say you're sorry. You wreck my painting and you say you're sorry. It doesn't mean anything."

"What else would you like me to say?" I asked.

"Maybe tell me why you did it," Bailey said.

I closed my eyes to try to put myself back in the moment in front of the canvas, and saw waves of light and color resolving themselves again in the dark behind my eyelids. "I knew you wanted your painting to be perfect and I thought you'd done it," I said. "I thought the seagull eye came out so well. But when I saw the piece of hair through my lens, it stood out like a sore thumb. I thought, 'I'll just fix it.'"

"But a piece of hair stuck in the paint isn't what's going to make or break a painting," she said.

"It would make or break a food photograph," I said. "I think that's where I messed up."

"No, Mom," she said. "You messed up in thinking you could touch my work. It's *my* work. It has to be totally my work. Your touching it was what ruined it."

"I guess that's the danger of being someone's mother. It's so easy to care too much about someone else's life."

"You totally stepped over the line."

"I know," I said. "I'm sorry. I truly am. But I've supported your art for twenty-three years. You're about to have the biggest night of your life, and I hope those twenty-three years count for something. I'd like to be able to come to the show to cheer you on."

"I'm not feeling very forgiving right now," she said.

"So you don't want me to come?"

"I never said that," she said.

"But if you can't even stand to be in my presence..."

"Fine, then," Bailey said. "Don't come to the show. Dad and I will go."

"Okay," I said. "But if you want to cut me out of your life like that, it doesn't make sense for you to work in my studio, and it doesn't make sense for me to do anything to help you or Alex Kepler with the enormous task you have before you. I hardly wanted an estate dumped in my lap right now, either."

"So sorry Grandpa's death is such an inconvenience to you," she said.

"Bailey, come on. We'll end up like those crazy families who have to go to court to decide who gets a rocking chair."

"I don't want Grandpa's furniture."

I closed my eyes, and this time, pine-tree needle designs swirled behind my lids like a kaleidoscope.

"Come on, Bailey. Give me something to give this guy. Anything."

She said nothing for a moment and then she said. "Okay. Fine. Tell Alex Kepler that I thought my grandfather was a genius, a hero, an American original. Tell him that I want all the iconic images—*American Buffalo* and *Morning Trout* and *Mount Whitney Sun-*

set—and I want all of them to be enormous so that when you're standing there you can feel exactly what it's like to be in the mountains with someone who loves them. I want them hung by time of day because that's the way Grandpa thought about things. I want a show that will blow all the poster buyers pretty much away."

I leaned forward and pulled back the black velvet curtain at the foot of the bed. I knew that if I looked out the window long enough, I would see a shooting star, a satellite moving across the sky, an airplane, a bat. The night sky in that part of the world is teeming with life. "Okay," I said—evenly, quietly; I was, after all the adult. "I'll tell him."

CHAPTER NINE

Flying into Los Angeles is a thrill no matter the time of year, the time of day, or the flight pattern. It's not like St. Martin, where you glide in straight over the water, or Gilbraltar, where the runway is literally built on the sea. But it has the absolute feel of being on the edge of a continent. From Salt Lake, you fly over Capitol Reef and the Escalante Wilderness. It's desolate out there. There's nothing but rock and an occasional road, a range of mountains, a few tiny towns. Then you come over the Angeles Crest and there's the enormous sprawl—the amazing reality of all those homes, all those cars, all those lights, and all those people packed into the tidal plain. As the plane edges toward the ocean, you can pick out the contours of the Santa Monica Bay, the harbor at Marina del Rey, the steam plant at El Porto, the piers of Manhattan, Hermosa, and Redondo Beach. As soon as the piers come into focus, you can spot our house. I always had the thought that if the plane just slowed down for a moment, I could gather up my books and magazines, my empty bottle of sparkling water, and just step off the wing and float down to my porch like Mary Poppins gliding into London.

Instead, of course, I waited for the plane to descend, to land, to taxi to the gate, and then I waited for all the people in front of me to gather their belongings and make their way off the plane, and then I waited at the airport curb amid the noise and the exhaust for Harrison to pick me up.

I spotted his car first—a deep sea-blue metallic BMW 550i, as solid, practical, and efficient as he was, a car that would never let you down—and as he moved out of the flow of traffic and pulled up to where I stood, I saw him. He was still wearing his clothes from the office—button-down shirt with a button-down collar, brown pants in a tropical-weight wool, Allen-Edmonds shoes built by hand with the same kind of precision as the car. I couldn't remember the last time I'd had to take a Town Car or taxi home from the airport. Harrison always picked me up. He was as reliable as clockwork, and while there was something deeply comforting about having someone be there for you so consistently, there was something disturbing about it, as well, because although Harrison would always love me, and would do anything to help me, he would never be able to get inside my skin. He would always be outside, other, and we would always be ultimately unknowable to each other.

I opened the car door and slipped into the front seat. Harrison leaned over and kissed me on the cheek. "How'd it go?" he asked, and with just those three words, the ambivalence I had been feeling toward him crystallized into something hard and ugly. *Oh, I had a great time,* I wanted to say. *Got a lot done, made friends with Alex Kepler, made up for Bailey's absence, made peace with my dad.*

"Fine," I said. "Did you get through your paperwork?"

He navigated the car through the traffic at LAX. "Most of it," he said.

I nodded. "That's good," I said. I had offered him nothing about what it had been like to start sifting through my father's estate, and he had offered me nothing in return about what it had been like to finalize the documents that would end an era of maple sugaring in his family. We had known each other so long that we could speak in shorthand now. There was no need to say anything real or revealing.

I remembered going to dinner one night in Burlington when Bailey was still an infant. We left her with Harrison's sister, and were giddy with excitement to have a long, leisurely night ahead of us. We ordered artichoke and lamb and chatted feverishly about our plans for our future, our thoughts about our new family. There was an older couple seated in the booth across from us—a professor and his wife, we guessed—and we noticed that they ordered exactly the same food that we did. During the course of the dinner, we kept watching them as if they had been placed there for our enjoyment like actors on a stage, but we noticed how they hardly spoke to each other. They sat in a pool of silence almost the entire evening, sipping their wine, taking bits of meat on their forks. "Poor old married couple have nothing to say to each other," Harrison whispered during dessert. "We'll never be like them," I whispered back, and seized his hand and kissed it.

Yet here we were, just like that old couple—saying nothing, doing nothing other than being present in each other's life. Was that enough? That day was one of the days I wasn't sure.

When we pulled into the garage, Harrison turned off the engine of the car, turned toward me, and, as if to prove that I had been wrong about being disconnected, said, "I heard Bailey yelling at you last night."

"I called to apologize," I said, grateful to be saying something of substance. "It didn't go very well. She doesn't want me to go to the show."

He nodded. "I was afraid of that."

"And I've been thinking about something she said to me that day in the studio. She said, 'Who are you to judge what makes art any good?' I've been thinking that maybe she's right. Maybe my dad has been right all this time, you know? That Bailey got the DNA and I didn't. Maybe that was the moment of truth right there in front of that seagull."

Harrison looked out the driver's side window, took a breath, and looked back. "People don't inherit the ability to make art, Claire. Maybe people can pick up on a passion, or learn a way of life, but this whole thing about DNA is just a pile of crap."

I cocked my head. "I just told you that I might have figured out that I'm not an artist, and you're going to sit there and tell me that what I'm feeling is a pile of crap?"

"I met you when you had a camera in your hands," Harrison said, "and I've lived with you for twenty-three years, most of which time you've had a camera in your hands. It's ridiculous to suddenly say that you don't have the right DNA to be an artist. A photographer is someone who takes photographs, and that makes you a photographer."

"But I may not be a very good one. That's what this is about."

"No," Harrison said. "You know what I think this is about?" He didn't wait for me to reply. "I think it's about the fact that you've spent your whole life wishing your father loved you better than he did."

"I do wish that," I said quietly. "I do."

"He loved you the best way he knew how, Claire. That's what we all do. He was a complicated and difficult guy who didn't have a lot of interest in sticking around and didn't have a lot of patience. But neither did my dad, and neither do a lot of other dads. You're fifty-four years old. I think it's time to get over it."

I opened the car door. "I'm not sure that's something you can just get over, Harrison."

"Well, I am," he said. "Because otherwise it's going to eat you alive."

There was a large manila envelope from Bridget in the stack of mail that had piled up for me while I was gone. Inside was the *Rolling Stone* issue she had mentioned—*Children of Rock: They Grew Up in the Shadow of Legends and Lived to Tell the Tale*—with a note written in her loopy cursive: *Thought you might like to see this*. The cover featured a photograph of Art Garfunkel's son, James Taylor's son, Marvin Gaye's daughter, and John Lennon's son Sean, a dark-haired young man in round glasses who looked like he had a shadow across his face. Could I imagine him opening his mouth to sing? I could, in fact, imagine it exactly. I could imagine him strumming a guitar alone in his bedroom, singing softly to the night, wondering if some of the stardust that had blessed his dad had fallen on him, too. I could also imagine John the father listening at the door, yearning for it to be true, and hoping against hope that it wasn't—because as magical as it is to have your child share your gifts and talents, what you really want as a parent is for your child to discover his own best way of being in the world and his own best way of connecting to other people.

I read the article about the strange and wonderful things the children of rock heard and saw as they grew up and when I was done, I went out to the flat files in my studio and pulled out some portfolios of my work. I had an entire drawer full of wedding photos, with cake after cake, and a large envelope that featured a

Thanksgiving dinner prepared by my friend Sonya, who at one time wanted to be a chef, but ended up being an executive assistant at Boeing. There were photos from the *Bon Appétit* years—mint sprigs and Christmas cookies, heirloom tomatoes and jambalaya—and one whole cabinet devoted to photos of Harrison and Bailey. I sifted through the photos, smiling at the memory of the time Harrison barbecued his first salmon, and the time Bailey went to the prom with the freckled boy who was a foot shorter than she was. Inside one large, thick envelope was an eleven-by-fourteen print of a picture of Bailey building a sand castle in the annual Manhattan Beach competition. People worked all day, sometimes in teams, creating elaborate sand sculptures of castles and villages, mermaids and dolphins. That year Bailey was twelve, and she insisted on working alone. She made a sleeping dragon with its head tucked under a wing and its tail curled up alongside its enormous, scaly body. The dragon was four feet wide and almost as tall as she was. In my photograph, she is lying on top of the beast, her long arms around its neck, pretending to sleep, as well. At the foot of the dragon lay the tools of her efforts—a plastic yellow bucket, a little red shovel, a tin funnel. The light of the late afternoon had washed the scene in gold—gold light, gold sand, golden child with golden hair. The photograph is so good that it almost seems as if I could reach out and brush the dusting of sand off Bailey's cheek.

I couldn't stand another day of walking on eggshells around my own daughter; I was desperate for some kind of resolution. I found Bailey in her room the next morning. There were clothes piled on the floor and outfits laid out on her bed, complete with underwear and jewelry.

"Hey," I said, from the doorway, "did you get your artist's statement done?"

"Yeah," she said, without looking at me.

"I told Alex what you said about Grandpa's work, and he was grateful for the direction."

"Good," she said.

"Are you planning out what to wear?"

"Yeah," she said.

She wasn't going to give me any ground. I took a step forward. "Bailey," I said, "I don't expect you to forgive me for what I did to your painting, and I suppose you don't have to talk to me if you can't stand it, but I'd really like to come to your show. I'd just really like to be there, especially since Grandpa's gone."

She shook her head. "He's dead, Mom. It's not like you can do anything about it."

"No," I said, "but at least you can have the rest of your family there."

"I don't think that's the best idea," she said. "I can't—" She started to say something, then stopped and sat down on the bed. "I can't look at you without seeing that painting. Every time I look at you, I see you standing with a brush in front of that painting. It just...it totally freaks me out."

She picked up a purple suede platform sling-back Mary Jane and slipped it onto her foot. "See, I hated that seagull," she said, "but I'd made peace with it. I mean, I'd decided that everything doesn't have to be perfect. I decided that it was good enough. Do you have any idea what a big deal that is for an artist? I mean, there are a million artists who paint stuff and keep it in their garage or their studio because they don't think it's good enough. Anyone can do that. But to be the kind of artist who says, 'I want my work to see the light of day and I think it's good enough to show'? That's huge."

I looked out the window at the beach, which was drenched in sunlight. I watched a man throw a blue Frisbee into the air like a boomerang; it came straight back to the exact place where he stood. Sometimes things worked exactly the way you wanted—kites flew, Frisbees came back—but often, they didn't. "I get it now," I said. "I get it, and I'm just...I'm so sorry. I completely understand why you wouldn't want me to come to your show. I can't undo what I did, but I guess I can stay away." I turned to leave just as Bailey picked up the second purple shoe.

"I guess you can come to the show," she said, "if you want."

It wasn't exactly a heartfelt invitation, but it was all I wanted. I turned back toward her, humble and elated. "Thank you," I said.

I walked into town to find something to wear. I passed the stationery store where a beautiful piece of marbled Italian paper was set out on a yellow painted table; a yarn shop where a basket was overflowing with cashmere the color of the Caribbean sea; a toy store with an elaborate wooden fairy tree house complete with a pulley and tiny wooden bucket; a shoe store with a pair of sandals whose tread was stamped with daisies; the bakery, where rosemary olive-oil bread had recently been taken out of the oven; and a T-shirt retailer who switched the palette of available colors every three months, reflecting the same kind of subtle sense of the progression of time that the natural world provides in places like Maine and Wyoming.

I stood on the corner of Manhattan Beach Boulevard for a few minutes watching people walk toward the roundhouse at the end of the pier. The glass of the windows of the hexagonal structure glinted in the sunlight and seemed to draw people toward it like a beacon. There was a bench I liked midway down the pier on the south side. You could sit there and look down the coast toward the cliffs of Palos Verdes. With the red tile roofs climbing into the sage-green hills and the blue water flashing below, the view from that bench looked exactly like the French Riviera.

I walked onto Highland Boulevard and stopped in front of a clothing store whose window featured a display in shades of brown and blue. There was a pair of wide-legged deep chocolate-brown linen pants paired with a white camisole and a flirty blue knit cardigan that was nipped in at the waist, flared at the wrists. I walked in and saw the ensemble on a rack against the wall. I touched the blue sweater. It felt cool and slippery, and when I checked the label, I saw that it was a silk, linen, and rayon blend.

"Would you like to try it on?" the saleslady asked. "I sold two of those sweaters this morning already." She had long black hair that looked as if it had been oiled. "One man bought it for his wife for her birthday and another woman bought it to wear to a party."

"My daughter's having a party," I said.

"Well, there you go." She stepped out from behind the counter and reached for the sweater. "These look great together," she said, grabbing a pair of pants. "What are you, a size eight?"

I nodded, took the clothes into the dressing room, and slipped them on. I felt instantly transformed. The stretchy camisole felt cool against my skin and the pants felt light as air. I normally wear blue jeans and black or white T-shirts or turtlenecks. They were a uniform, something I didn't have to think about every day. I turned to view myself in the mirror, and noted the way the sweater flared at the wrists. It had a row of fabric-covered buttons down the front, which stopped at the waist, and from that line the sweater flared out, as well.

I stepped out of the dressing room so the saleslady could appraise me. "See?" she said. "It's a magic sweater. It looks fabulous."

I bought the entire ensemble, with a hammered-silver necklace to match. The tab came to $427, and something about the expense seemed entirely justified. Perhaps in order to be forgiven, I had to be wearing a fabulous pair of pants. Perhaps in order to stop feeling doubt, I had to be wearing a silk knit sweater. Maybe what had been holding me back from seeing was how I saw myself and maybe that could change in an instant, if only I had the right clothes.

When I got home, I put the outfit on again to make

sure I hadn't made a mistake. Seconds later, Bailey tapped on my bedroom door.

"Do you know where Dad is?" she asked.

"I haven't seen him," I said.

She hesitated a moment. "Those colors clash with your gray hair," she said. "You should stick with black."

I returned the clothes the next day, and the necklace, too. The same saleslady was there, and I was so mindful of her previous enthusiasm that I crafted a lie. "I learned that the reception's going to be outside, so I need something warmer, in case it's cold."

She smiled. She said it was no problem. She did not try to point out that no one ever wears more than a sweater in Southern California in the spring.

I called Bridget that night. "I have nothing to wear to Bailey's opening," I said.

"Do you even own anything that's not black?"

"I have things that are gray."

"So what's the problem? You wear black pants, a gray sweater. A nice pair of shoes."

I looked at my hands. "The problem," I said, "is that I've already pissed her off. I don't want to embarrass her, too."

"How would that happen?"

"If I look too young or too much like I'm someone's mom or like I'm a person who is trying too hard or like I'm a person who expects her paintings to do well or who doesn't expect her paintings to do well. There's a very narrow range of options available to me. Invisible would be best."

"Oh," Bridget said, as if the entire workings of the universe were suddenly clear. "You know what happened to me the other day? I went to a hockey party, and I stood in the doorway of this room filled with eighteen-year-old boys and their parents, and not one person looked at me. Not one person said, 'Hi, Mrs. Tate,' or 'Aren't you Cole's mom?' or 'Don't you work at the Bean?' I swear I had a moment where I thought, 'Whoa! I'm invisible.'"

"Maybe you're further along the spectrum than I am," I said. "I just feel faded and dull. Maybe invisible is what comes next."

"We'll be like the furniture," Bridget said. "Like a bunch of old chairs just sitting there in the middle of every room."

I laughed. "Speaking of furniture, do you remember that guy I went on that blind date with sophomore year? Peter Couch?"

"You wanted to marry him after that night, but then he never called."

"He disappeared off the face of the earth is more like it, and totally broke my heart."

"What about him?"

"I've never stopped thinking about him."

"No shit? You pine for Peter Couch?"

"No, I don't *pine* for him. I just wonder what happened to him, you know? Whether he became a Hollywood producer like he said he was going to be, or if he ended up being a tax attorney or a tennis pro. And I'd really like to know why he never called when we had such a good time that night."

"You do see what point this makes, don't you?" Bridget said. "If you're still thinking about Peter Couch thirty-four years after one measly date, then imagine the beach-head you have in *my* brain. Invisible isn't happening."

CHAPTER TEN

I *was scheduled* to shoot billboards of Limoncello, an Italian after-dinner drink, on Wednesday and Thursday. We only needed three shots, and we were going to do them in the garden on a wrought-iron table in the sun. Frosted glass, the crystalline yellow liquid, a few twists of lemon peel. It was an easy job and I felt good about it; I was certain that I would be back on top of my game. Peter came with the computer, the camera, and his laid-back style. I gave him a big hug and said, "Have I ever told you how much I enjoy working with you, Peter?"

"No," he said, "not lately. Bring it on."

"I just love how you always show up on time and how nothing fazes you and how you always make it seem like we have all day to do whatever we have to do."

He grinned. "The sun's shining; they say the surf will be good tomorrow. So we do have all day."

Francesca brought the glass—crates of long-necked bottles and classic olive-oil bottles with hinged stoppers, and jugs and jars. I helped her unload the treasure and we debated whether we thought a yellow napkin folded behind the shot would enhance the yellow of the liquor or detract from it. "Let's go without," I finally said. "We've got great light today, and I love the soft yellow all on its own."

The art director, a bald guy named Leo, began to move the wrought-iron table around my garden to find the best location. We ended up placing it near a lime tree and a trellis of jasmine that smelled sublime.

"It's like the tropics," Leo said. "We should have rum drinks for lunch!"

Francesca poured the Limoncello into the bottles we selected, and she and Leo arranged them on the wrought-iron table in the sun. The colors and shapes were strong, the light was perfect, nothing was going to go wrong today. "Don't move a thing," I said, but before I had finished speaking, a swarm of yellow jackets descended on our tableau, and on us. There were yellow jackets in my hair, on my clothes, on my shoes. We retreated to the studio and sent an assistant for bug spray. When she returned, we went back to try the shot again. We got everything ready to go—the best whorls of the wrought iron, the twist of lemon peel curling just so, the tall frosted bottle devoid of fingerprints, with light refracting perfectly through the yellow liquid— and then we sent the shot to the client to get the final okay.

While we waited, the yellow jackets kept buzzing around our heads. They sounded like jet planes; they advanced like an army. By the time we got the okay to take the shot, we were nearly delirious with their presence. Peter and Francesca stood just outside the frame of the photo, waving dishtowels to keep the bugs off our tableau. I crouched behind the camera and watched as a yellow jacket landed on the lemon peel. In my magnified view, the yellow-and-black patterns on his long body looked as big as the bands on a Navajo rug. His legs were splayed and barbed, his wings were veined and shiny, his huge black eyes looked at me with an ancient ignorant dullness. I took a deep breath and pushed the air out, then sucked in more air as quickly as I could—in, out; in, out.

"Get away!" I yelled, but the yellow jacket stuck his

proboscis into the lemon peel, and I could see where it pierced the white membrane, where he would leave a hole, and I knew that we would have to repeel a dozen more lemons to get another curl that good. "Get away!"

I raced forward, flailing my arms, then seized a fly-swatter and swiped at the one grotesque intruder. My plastic paddle sideswiped the glass bottle, knocking it to the table. It sprayed its sticky lemon liquor all over the table, all over the yellow napkin folded just so, all over the ground. A thousand yellow jackets descended on the feast.

Francesca screamed. Leo cursed. The color drained from my face and I stood frozen in place, dumbfounded by what I had just done. Peter came over, put his arm around me, and led me away from the scene the way you would direct a small child who had just finished having a tantrum. He sat me down inside the studio.

"What's going on?" he asked simply.

I looked at him and shook my head. I could already taste the salt of my tears. "I don't think I can do this anymore," I whispered.

"Do what?"

"Take picture after picture of this food or that food. Nothing looks right anymore. And the other thing is? None of it seems to matter. Don't you ever wonder what the hell we're doing out here? Seeking perfection so someone will buy a bottle of lemon-flavored after-dinner drink? It's crazy. There are eight people here today to take three photographs."

"Nine," Peter said, "if you count the caterer."

"But don't you ever wonder about it, Peter?"

He shrugged. "The way I figure it," he said, "it's just a job. Same as hauling brick or cutting lumber. If people are willing to pay, it matters enough."

"I don't know," I said. "I just don't know."

"Maybe you should take a break," Peter said. "Take some time to chill out, you know?"

I nodded. "A break would be good," I said. "Maybe after the cupcake shoot."

"Take a few weeks or a month."

I nodded. "I'll talk to Harrison," I said. "And ask him to build in a break."

CHAPTER ELEVEN

I *ended up* wearing exactly what Bridget predicted I would wear to Bailey's exhibition—black pants, black mules, a gray sweater. The pants, however, were beautifully cut silk jersey, the mules were European calfskin, and the sweater was a knee-length wool-and-mohair coat with triangular hand-painted ceramic buttons.

"You look good," Harrison said, when I came out of the bathroom.

I put my arms around his neck. "You, too," I said. He was wearing a cashmere blazer, a white collared shirt.

His hair, fully gray now, was cropped close to his head. He smelled like soap and toothpaste. He smelled good.

"This doesn't feel how I always imagined it would," I said. "I feel a bit nauseous, actually."

"She's not even going to notice that we're there," he said.

I shrugged. "I guess not," I said. "I just hope she has a good night. I mean, I hope she doesn't end up disappointed."

He laughed. "Because disappointment is so alien to the life of an artist? You haven't been paying much attention to your own family."

"It's not that," I said. "It's just that I can't suddenly stop worrying about her. Just because she's about to get a graduate degree doesn't mean I can stop worrying."

He picked up his wallet, palmed his car keys. All he'd ever wanted was to be a better father than his father had been to him, but he somehow knew that love—whether it was a parent for a child, a husband for a wife, or a person for her art—was always imperfect. "You should try," he said.

He was on his way out the door when I spoke. He was the person who knew me better than anyone else, who wanted what was good for me more than anyone else. "Harrison?" I said, and he stopped and turned. "I'm not sure I know how to try."

"To stop worrying?"

I nodded.

"You could start by trusting her," he said. "She knows exactly what she's doing. I think that's one of the reasons people respond so strongly to her work. There's such a sense of inevitability about it, you know? She paints with so little doubt."

"That kind of faith is so alien to me right now," I said, shaking my head. "I don't trust anything about anything anymore. That's part of what's been going on at work. It's like I can't see straight. I can't think straight. I question every little speck of dust. It's like some strange mental affliction."

Harrison stepped back and took me in his arms. I leaned my head onto his shoulder and let it rest there. I let my arms hang down his sides, and let him just hold me. "I was thinking that it might help if I took a little break from work," I said. "I was thinking that it might be good for me to step back for a few weeks, maybe once the cupcake book is done."

"If you think it would help," he said, "then of course that's what you should do. But I've been talking to California Pizza Kitchen about their new menu, and a creamery that's opening in Santa Barbara. They both want to shoot in June."

I pulled back so I could look into his face. "You're

amazing," I said, "but the idea of shooting butter just makes my stomach turn."

"Okay," he said. "I'll freeze your calendar after the cupcake shoot. I'll freeze it through June."

"Thank you," I said, and kissed him, and felt that everything was going to be okay.

The show was held in the Williamson Gallery—a beautiful open space with large rectangular skylights. There were bottles of wine and water at a table outside the door, and platters of grapes and orange cheese cut into cubes. People gathered around the tables—a woman whose large tattoo of an Irish cross was framed by the open back of her sundress, a man in a goatee, groups of students in jeans and army-green jackets—and inside, the rooms were buzzing like a theater on opening night.

The first exhibition featured a pie plate impaled on the wall with a butcher knife and a framed painting that was done in blood. Almost no one stopped to look at this work. They walked by, heads down, eyes averted. The second exhibition was a series of photographs that had been taken in a paint store. There was a shot of the paint chips lined up in their graduated rows; a shot of the machine that mixed the paint, coated in several years' worth of drips; and a zoomed-in shot of a paintbrush that made it look like a sheaf of wheat. They were alluring and original and people stood in front of them talking animatedly about their experiences at paint stores, and with paint chips, and with painting their homes.

I imagined what it would be like to have my own work hung on the wall next to the paint-store photos— six badly lit shots of gourmet chocolate displayed with Harry Winston jewels. People would, perhaps, stop and nod in recognition. *Haven't we seen something like that before?* they might whisper. *Doesn't that remind you of something* Gourmet *once did?* But would they stop and consider the slant of light? Would they marvel at how the chocolate glistened just so? Would they take anything away other than a vague sense of having seen something similar somewhere? I doubted it. Next to the graduate student who had done a study of paint chips and made a statement about the presence of color in our lives, my photos would look exactly like what they were: client-directed creations designed to sell merchandise.

Bailey's work was on the back wall. From across the large, open space, the paintings were far more commanding than they had been in the small room at the back of our studio. They needed the air around them, as if they were creatures that breathed. As you approached the paintings, you could almost hear the sound of the surf. You could almost feel the hot sand beneath your feet.

I tried to keep my eyes from moving to the painting of the wave. There was a knot of people in front of it, and another two groups a few feet back.

I veered toward Bailey. She was standing to one side of her work, talking to two men—one bald, in jeans and a V-neck sweater, the other taller, in jeans and a blazer. The men were older than the students. Their jeans were better cut, their sweater and coat were made of wool so fine it seemed to shine under the bright lights. Bailey flicked her eyes in our direction, but she made no movement to break out of the group, and seemed to be very intent as she spoke to the man in the blazer. Harrison and I stood a respectful distance away, holding our wine, looking around, feeling out of place. I heard Bailey say the words *linen canvas* and *anger so hot it shatters*.

Bailey had ironed her hair so that it looked like corn silk sweeping across her forehead and catching behind her ear. Around her neck she wore a piece of blue sea glass on a silver chain. She had found that piece of glass—a chunk about the size of a quarter, shaped like a heart—the summer she turned eight, and she considered it a talisman of good luck. She was wearing cropped black pants, a tight purple tissue T-shirt, and her purple heels. I realized how very little difference it made to anyone what I was wearing.

"That bald man looks like Bruce Willis," I said quietly. "Do you think it could be Bruce Willis?"

"You mean Jason Alexander," Harrison said.

"No, Bruce Willis, *Die Hard.*"

"I don't know," Harrison said, shaking his head, and then, "Bailey looks good."

She flashed her eyes toward us again, turned back to the two men, and then said, "Here are my parents."

The men turned and smiled, though not broadly, not in any way that could be seen as welcoming.

We stepped toward the group. "Mom, Dad," Bailey said, "this is David Geffen and George Fleischman, his art adviser. These are my parents, Harrison and Claire Brown."

We leaned forward, shook hands. Pleasantries were exchanged about Bailey's painting and the show. The whole time I was thinking, *David Geffen the movie mogul, the theater patron, the art collector?* and then I looked at Bailey—her blond hair shining, her eyes reflecting light—and I remembered that she was my father's granddaughter. There was a logic to her life that wasn't governed by the laws that ruled over mere mortals. I knew that the answer was yes. It *was* David Geffen the movie mogul, the theater patron, the art collector, and the stars had been aligned in just the right way to bring him to this small show tonight, to put him in front of Bailey's work, to be the catalyst for something big to happen in her life. It made perfect sense.

I wanted to calmly tell Mr. Geffen that there had been another canvas in the series. I wanted to tell him that it had been beautiful. I wanted to tell him that the wave that broke out of the bounds of its frame was my fault, but I just stood there, my palms sweating, the wine trembling in my glass, until George Fleischman took out a business card and handed it to Bailey. "Give me a call," he said. And then to me and to Harrison, he said, "Good night. Enjoy the show."

When they turned the corner and disappeared from sight, Bailey pressed her face into her hands as if she were trying to hold back tears. She sucked in a breath of air and then looked up at us. "That was David *Geffen*," she said. "I have to go find Nora"—her professor and adviser, a woman who, like me, only wore black, but who, unlike me, had an opinion that mattered to my daughter. She spun away from us, then turned back and over her shoulder called, "Did you see the flowers Robin's holding? They're from Nora."

We saw Robin, Bailey's roommate, who still had a year before her own MFA show, standing like a bridesmaid in the group that stood in front of Bailey's wave painting. She was wearing black skinny jeans with holes at the knees, a Harley-Davidson T-shirt, and in her arms, she was holding a bouquet of enormous pink stargazer lilies.

I'd forgotten flowers. I had nothing to offer. Even my apology had been rejected. But I had my Canon camera. I took it out of my purse, turned it on, and raised it to my eye. I was going to take a picture of Robin and the flowers and the knot of people, but before I could adjust the speed, a guard came up to me and tapped me on the shoulder.

"I'm sorry, ma'am," he said. "No photography is allowed in the gallery."

I opened and closed my mouth like a fish. "No photography?" I asked.

"That's right," the guard said. "I'm sorry."

"She's my daughter," I said, looking around so that I could point to Bailey and claim some kind of special exemption, but she was nowhere to be seen.

CHAPTER TWELVE

The next morning, there was a write-up about the MFA exhibition in the *L.A. Times*. It was buried on page 5 of the calendar section, two columns about four inches long, with the headline NEW CROP OF HOT ARTISTS. The reporter had missed the fact that one of the country's foremost private collectors of contemporary art had slipped into the show to see which young artists might be worth watching, but she managed to identify Bailey as the granddaughter of legendary landscape photographer Paul Switzer. Now Bailey would never have a moment to be just Bailey Brown, painter, but would always be Bailey Brown, granddaughter of legendary landscape photographer Paul Switzer. I wanted to discount every word the reporter wrote after that, but at the end of the paragraph discussing Bailey's work—the technical virtuosity, the feeling of move-ment—the reporter wrote, *It will be a distinct pleasure to watch Ms. Brown paint more and more subtle can-vases and to relax into the arms of her own competence.* I thought that was lovely.

I could tell that no one in the house had read the newspaper before me that morning. The sports section was still neatly folded, the comics still lay undisturbed. I took the calendar section and walked it back to the studio, where Harrison and Bailey were on speaker-phone with Nora. I stood in the doorway and listened to Nora's voice flood the room. "It's not typical," she said, "for an artist to represent her own work, but I don't see any reason why your dad can't return the call in this case, Bailey."

"What's going on?" I mouthed, when Harrison turned to look at me.

He held up his finger—just a minute—then turned toward the phone and asked Nora a question about writing a contract.

I looked at Bailey and held out my hands—*What's*

going on?—but she just shook her head. I felt like I was watching my dad and Bailey paint on the banks of the Teton River, or Harrison and my dad pack up to go off to commune with the fish. I reached around Harrison, who was sitting in my chair, and pulled a hot-pink Post-it note from the cube on my desk. I scrawled three exclamation points, pasted it on top of the newspaper article, set the newspaper on the desk in front of Bailey, and fled.

Everyone in my family is a runner, but we all run in different ways. Harrison runs religiously every morning, two miles south and two miles back to the house. On weekends, he runs even farther, and he never runs on the sand. Bailey runs long-distance, also on cement, sometimes north and sometimes south. She ran on the cross-country team in high school and she often runs the same workouts she learned in those years. She'll go all the way up to Marina del Rey to the breakwater, or down to the Palos Verdes Beach Club where the sand gives way to rock as the peninsula juts out into the water. I like to run on the sand, barefoot. I go until my calves start to hurt, which can happen in half a mile or three miles, depending on my mood, depending on the day. I often walk home. That morning, I ran south from the house, two miles down to the Hermosa Beach pier, as fast as I could. I ran through the wash of the waves, and water sprayed up at me, soaking my shorts, the front of my shirt, and my face. I didn't bother to stop to wipe it off.

When I got to Hermosa, my heels hurt, my calves ached, and my hamstrings burned. It felt good to have such a simple, physical problem that would be solved by some simple, practical remedies such as a bit of stretching, a little time.

When I got back to the house, I came up to the back door, sat on a chaise longue, and checked my feet for tar. There were globs on both my heels. I opened the lid of the stainless-steel bucket where we keep turpentine and rags and began to scrub off the black gunk. While I was scrubbing, a young man walked by on the bike path on the other side of the low wall that separates our patio from the path. He was carrying a longboard, which is not an easy thing to do, and as he paused to heft the board a little higher on his hip, he caught my eye in that way that demands you say something polite and noncommittal.

"Tar's bad right now, isn't it?" I said.

"It's the worst I can remember," he said.

That would have been it—the whole of our exchange,

the extent of our relationship—except that at that moment Bailey leaned out of the French doors.

"Phone, Mom," she said, holding the phone out in her hand.

The young man with the surfboard smiled at her and she smiled back. He was tan, with blond hair that sprang from his head in tiny ringlets, like golden springs. He had broad shoulders, an easy smile.

"We were talking about the tar," I said, by way of explaining what I was doing talking to a handsome passerby who was closer to her age than to mine. I stood and stepped toward the door.

"The tar's horrible this year," Bailey said, handing me the phone and smoothing her hair behind her ear. Instead of stepping aside to let me in, she stepped outside into the sunlight.

I took the phone, moved inside the doorway, and said hello. It was Alex Kepler.

"There's a reporter from the *Chicago Tribune* who's digging around for a story about the destroyed negatives," he said. "They seem to think there might be a lawsuit for control of the negatives. They got an anonymous tip."

"A lawsuit?" I said.

"Do you know of any disgruntled associates your dad might have had, any spurned lovers, jilted business partners? Is there anyone who might have had a claim to those negatives, or to the ones that survived?"

"I have no idea," I said.

"Do you know why your dad destroyed the negatives?"

"He destroyed the negatives to increase their value," I said. "It's not rocket science."

"There's no reason to get upset," Alex said. "But I have reason to believe that he might have had other motives. That there might be some people who could have a claim to what he ruined and what he left behind."

"Who would make that kind of claim?"

"That's what I'm asking you."

Something clicked in my brain about what Alex was insinuating. "Are you saying that you think I would sue for control of the negatives?" I asked.

"I'm trying to piece together the story of the bequest your father made to the Center for Creative Photography," he said, "and the story of who might get in the way of it is an important piece of the puzzle."

I began to pace across the room. Alex Kepler was dangerously close to disturbing the peace I had finally made with Bailey. "Look," I said. "I would be a fool to sue my own child. I don't need the money, and I sure as hell don't need the guilt."

I slammed down the phone and growled.

"You okay, Mom?" Bailey called. She was still outside on the patio, and those were the first kind words she had said to me in two weeks. She made it sound as if she was worried about me, as if she couldn't bear the thought of my being so upset. She and I would ride together into Driggs and run Alex Kepler out of town, out of Paul Switzer's estate. We would claim our legacy together, and relegate Alex to the role of administrative assistant.

I went to the door. The surfer was sitting sideways on the wall. His board was propped up next to him. Bailey was sitting a few feet away on one of the teak chaises, the slender calf of her left leg pulled up onto the cushions. All her life, Bailey had been like the sun, and boys—who had now become men—were her planets. I had watched them rotating, revolving, angling toward her, and though she shined, though she gave off light and heat and some-thing they all needed, she never moved toward them. She never budged. Even the men she dated, she held at a dis-tance. It always amazed me that the spiky-haired artists and the studious guys from Harrison's business-school seminars and her friends from college who were back in town trying to make it as screenwriters couldn't feel it.

Who's to say why any one person attracts or repels us any more than another? Who can say what, exactly, it is that changes in the air and the atmosphere? All I knew was that with this guy on the wall, something was very different. Bailey faced him. She leaned toward him. She seemed ready to leap up and follow him wherever it was he was going.

I stopped short in the doorway. "I'm fine," I said, in a voice that sounded wounded, even to me. I couldn't hide my surprise or my disappointment.

"You were yelling," Bailey said.

"Was I?" I asked, as if I'd been caught doing something unseemly. "I didn't mean to. Sorry. Excuse me." I retreated back inside, wondering what Bailey and the surfer could be talking about. What Bailey talked about, mostly, was color. She talked about the gradation in the sky at sunset, the quality of purple in the white of the clouds, the way the sand on a certain beach had more ocher than gray, why the sage green on the border of the rug looked best against the clay of the tile on the floor, how black looked better on me than brown and blue. On that morning, she had been courted by powerful people in the world of art. She'd possibly already made deals, set a course for her future. On a day like that, what could she have to say to a stranger who happened to pause on the bike path in front of our house?

I was standing in front of the refrigerator finishing a glass of water and still musing over these questions when Bailey came inside.

"So who was on the phone who pissed you off so much?" she asked.

"Alex Kepler," I said, grateful for my chance to be alone with Bailey and to connect with her. "He's angling to make some big discovery, or at least big headlines. I don't trust him as far as I could throw him."

"Don't worry," she said. "He can't breathe without me giving him the okay."

I laughed. "That's true," I said, and then, because I was feeling the rush of being in Bailey's good favor again and because there were so many things, still, that needed to be said, I dared to say one more thing. I chose not to use the moment to say that I was sorry, again, for what I had done to her painting; I felt certain that she already knew I would take back that dab of paint for anything. "I never got to tell you how proud I was of you at the show," I said. "Your work is spectacular, Bailey. It looks so powerful on the wall and I hope it will hang in galleries and museums all over the world one day. But even more than the paintings themselves, I was just so proud of who you are and how hard you've worked and how far you've come. The whole time I was at the show, I kept thinking about you when you got your first box of crayons—the sixty-four-color box with the sharpener—and how you used to spend all afternoon sharpening and sorting the colors. I'd try to read you a story or get you to build something with blocks, but you'd just go right back to that box of crayons. Do you remember the night you insisted on sleeping with it?"

"Oh my God!" she said, laughing. "It fell open and I crushed all the crayons. I cried for a week. It was such a nightmare!"

I leaned forward and smoothed a piece of hair behind her ear. "You're an amazing person and I'm lucky to be your mother."

"Thanks, Mom," she said. "Did Dad tell you what happened this morning?"

I shook my head no. The morning had already been so full—of the article in the newspaper and the young man on the beach and the phone call from Alex.

"Mr. Fleischman called Nora this morning. David Geffen wants to see how the painting looks on his wall to see if he wants to buy it."

It took about three beats for me to grasp what she was saying, and then I gasped. "Are you kidding?"

"I guess collectors do that now, you know? Try to swoop in and buy stuff from young artists before anyone else knows about them."

"Bailey," I said, "this is fantastic!" I threw my arms

around her and felt the solidness of her body, the warmth, and it felt exactly like a miracle to be standing with her in a moment of celebration that just a few weeks ago had seemed like a distant shore we would never reach.

"I'm nervous," she said. "I mean, it's one thing to win a student contest or to have a painting hanging in a show at a school gallery, but to think of my painting on a major collector's wall? What if it looks like crap once it's hanging there? What if they change their minds and say, 'Oh, sorry, actually your painting sucks now that we really think about it.'"

"They won't think that," I said, "These people know good art when they see it, and you make good art."

"I guess," she said.

"Did you read the *Times* piece?" I asked, and felt a rush of joy that here I was, offering Bailey solace and advice. Here I was, being her mother.

She smiled—a small turning-up of her nose and lips.

"Did you hear what that writer said?" I asked, " 'It will be a pleasure to watch her relax into the arms of her own competence.' The key word here is *relax*. Well, that and *competence*. You're very good, Bailey. You're very, very good and you should never doubt it." I was thankful that Bailey had no idea what had been going on with my own work. What a hypocrite she'd think I was if she knew that doubt was what I awoke to every day and went to sleep with every night.

"But what if the only reason they think my work is any good is because I'm Paul Switzer's grandchild?"

I thought back to the *Rolling Stone* cover story. "You were born into his family," I said, "for better or for worse. Some people might say it's actually harder to follow in a family member's footsteps than it would be to forge your own way. Whether or not that's true, the only thing you can do is to make the best art you know how, put it out in the world, and hope that people connect to it. Whatever happens once it's out there—whether people love your work or hate it, or why they love it or hate it—isn't your concern."

"Did you always want to be a food photographer?" she asked, "Or did you ever think about taking landscapes?"

"I tried landscapes once when I was a teenager," I said. "It didn't go so well. I got into food because of people's wedding cakes. I thought I could make them look better than they actually tasted in real life. It was a challenge. It was fun."

She nodded. "There's a guy in the class behind me who paints food," she said. "But they're strange old-fashioned still lifes. They're totally irrelevant."

"Everyone's got to do what they've got to do," I said, and then when I realized that it was lunchtime and that Bailey had stayed near me of her own volition, I said, "Hey—would you like a celebratory salad for lunch?"

She shook her head. "I'm going up to change," she said. "I'm meeting that guy at the pancake house."

"The guy with the tar?" I asked, feeling a sudden stab of jealousy. On this day of reconciliation, she was going to eat lunch with a stranger she met on the beach and not with me? Was it that fleeting, my place in the sun?

"His name's Tommy," she said, with a sense of delight and ownership that seemed far larger than warranted. "Tommy St. John."

They went out to lunch, they went out to dinner, they went out to lunch again the next day, and before they parted that afternoon, they talked about going for a run on Saturday, which was the next sliver of time Tommy had off work. He was a grip—the guy in charge of getting the camera where it needed to go on a movie set— and often worked fifteen-hour days.

"You can't see him on Saturday," I said, willing my voice to stay even-keeled. "Alex Kepler is expecting us in Driggs. I've been promising you for weeks. If you don't show up, he might explode."

"Mom," she said, as if I were a complete idiot for not seeing the way things were, "I really like this guy. Alex Kepler is going to have to wait."

CHAPTER THIRTEEN

The week that Tommy St. John stopped to chat on our patio about tar, I had a meeting with the cookbook editor from Martha Stewart. Her name was Michelle Dorsey, and she was scheduled to come to the studio at nine on Wednesday. She arrived exactly on time—an efficient bundle of energy who set me on edge the moment I met her.

"Claire!" she said, air-kissing both my cheeks, and stepping into the studio before I had a chance to invite her in. "We're all so pleased you're working on this project. You ready to get started?"

I showed her to the big conference table and perched on a chair nearest the door, to at least preserve the illusion that I could bolt outside at a moment's notice. Michelle had a binder full of recipes, with proposed layouts. She had worked out the type, the headlines, the precise way that each cupcake was going to appear—on a plate, on a platter, on a stand, on a tray, in a basket, with other cupcakes all around it like a cupcake convention, or all by itself like a monument to sugar and childhood.

I pretended to listen, but kept a running mantra in my head, *It's Martha Stewart, it's Martha Stewart.* Martha had transformed the way that food is photographed. Before Martha, food was often faked and stylized. What appeared to be ice cream was really lard and food coloring. What appeared to be water drops were really drops of glycerin. Martha changed all that. Put real berry pie on a pretty table in the garden, she commanded. Put real roasted potatoes on a pretty table in the kitchen. The way Martha presented food put it into the context of a story, and people love stories. Other publications began to follow suit. I watched the revolution from the test kitchens of *Bon Appétit.* I watched the art director pore over Martha's magazine, listened to him discussing the layouts with the photography editors. And soon enough, we were shooting like Martha, too.

To actually *work* for Martha Stewart was something I'd hardly dared dream, but one of the things Harrison did when he agreed to work with me was to insist that I write down my dreams in specific detail. It was agonizing, but one of the most persistent thoughts was this: I want to do an entire cookbook with Martha Stewart. My mother loved to cook and to bake, and like many New England mothers, she loved to can fruit at the end of summer when you could get bushels of blueberries for a few dollars at a roadside stand. She would sing while she canned—*"I'm gonna wash that man that right out of my hair,"* and *"I found my thrill on Blueberry Hill"*—and she would say, "Someday I'm going to write all these recipes down and make a cookbook."

After my dad left, she stopped singing and canning and worked at being a model citizen in a town that had rarely known a single mom. She worked more than full-time at the engineering office, was the first one to volunteer to make costumes for the middle-school play, kept our house spotless and our lawn raked, and made sure that I did my homework, brushed my hair, and always said "please" and "thank you." I sometimes got out the flour and the butter, thinking that if she just got her hands into the dough again, she would remember its pleasures, but her pie making became like everything else in her life: a chore that needed to be checked off a list. I often imagined that when I left for college, she would regain her sense of playfulness. Maybe she would fall in love again, celebrate the abundance of blueberries, become a woman who still sang the hits of Rodgers and Hammerstein—but she got sick before she got the chance. When I added *shoot a Martha Stewart cookbook* to my list of goals for Harrison, I imagined that it would be both the culmination of a glorious career and a shining tribute to my mom. Now that I was actually about to start the dream project, however, it felt like the only thing that stood between me and freedom. As soon as I was done with the cupcakes, I could take the break I so sorely needed.

While Michelle talked about mood and feeling and the way she wanted to see each photo cropped, I pictured zooming in on a gaudy bright pink frosted cupcake with pastel-colored nonpareils and I could imagine us all fussing with each of the crumbs on the plate for one hour, then two, three hours, then four. I pictured someone worrying about a sprinkle, another person concerned about the way the frosting curled back on itself. I saw the way the food stylist's assistant would follow the stylist around, her hand on her tool belt, ready to whip out a Handi Wipe the minute her boss got a bit of frosting on her hand.

"Do you have any thoughts?" Michelle asked at the end of her presentation, and I realized with dismay that I had been paying no attention to her plan.

"No," I said quickly, to cover my mistake, "it sounds like a solid plan." I figured that I had plenty of time to look through her binders after she left, get a sense of how things were going to go, and be ready to start the shoot when I returned from Driggs.

"So you'll book Peter, Jeff, and Tony?" she asked, rising from her chair and moving toward the door.

"Absolutely," I said.

"And I'll contact the prop stylist and start calling things in," Michelle said. "I saw bamboo baskets the other day. They were round and shallow and they fit perfectly with our color palette."

"Perfect," I said.

Finally, to my great relief, she said good-bye and walked out the door.

I was standing at the kitchen counter studying cup-cake recipes—gingerbread with cream-cheese frosting, red velvet with vanilla frosting, pumpkin spice, lemon twist—when Harrison burst through door, set down his briefcase, pumped his fist in the air as if he'd just made a touchdown, and said, "Where's Bailey?"

I stood, alarmed by his urgency. "Upstairs, I think. Getting ready to go out with Tommy. What's going on?"

He ignored me, and bounced to the bottom of the stairway. "Bailey!" he called. "Bailey!"

A door opened upstairs, and she appeared at the top of the stairs. She placed both hands on the wrought-iron railings and leaned over. "What's going on?"

"*Art Forum* called to interview you," he said.

Bailey came down the stairs, two at a time. "No shit?"

"No shit," he said. "But do you know why they called?"
She shook her head.

"Geffen's dealer made an offer. He wants the painting, and his dealer wants to talk to you about a solo show at New York gallery."

Harrison turned to see my reaction. I beamed, as best as I was able. It was, after all, staggeringly good news. Bailey would never need to do anything besides make art. Just like that, she would be a star. But I couldn't help thinking how nature abhors a vacuum: I had asked Harrison to stop booking me work, and almost instantly, he had started booking work for Bailey. I wanted to say, *No, wait! I changed my mind!*—because I recalled a very similar scene when I first sent off my portfolio to *Bon Appétit*. Harrison had helped me prepare the photographs and he'd edited my cover letter, and he'd come home expectant every night to see if I'd heard a response, and on the day when I said, *They offered me an internship,* he whooped and hollered and danced around this very same staircase. He was something of a genius at helping people get what they wanted. It was no wonder that he'd built a career helping people follow their dreams, because he made you feel as if anything was possible. I'm not proud to admit that at the moment of my daughter's greatest triumph, I felt a pang of grief that I had just handed back the right to feel the bright light of his inspiration.

Bailey leaped up and threw herself into her dad's arms. He spun her and set her down on the floor. She raced toward me, threw her arms around my neck, buried her face against my shoulder and squealed, and then released me.

"He wants to *buy* it?"

Harrison nodded.

"And I get a solo show? I can paint whatever I want?"

"You won the golden ticket, Sunshine."

Bailey raced back toward Harrison and flung her

arms around him. "Thank you, Daddy," she said. "Thank you so much."

I forced my feet to move across the floor so that I could wedge myself into the celebration. "Congratulations, sweetheart," I said to Bailey, and kissed her on the cheek. "And to you, too," I said to Harrison, and kissed him, too. They received my small gestures of praise with smiles and nods, but I could feel the raw fact that I was outside their circle of delight, and it felt devastating.

CHAPTER FOURTEEN

Alex came to the front door of the house as soon as he heard the wheels of my 4Runner on the gravel of the driveway. It was April, and although the snow was mostly gone, it was still cold.

"Where's Bailey?" he asked, when I emerged from the car alone.

I shook my head. "She couldn't make it."

"She said she was coming," Alex said. "I talked to her on Tuesday."

"Something came up," I said. "An emergency. She wanted me to say she's sorry."

Alex closed his eyes, turned away from me, and took a few steps toward the Tetons. His shoes crunched on the gravel of the driveway. He breathed, looked at the sky, and then turned back toward me. "Do you have any idea," he said, "of the magnitude of responsibility your father left to Bailey? Of the reputations and the revenue resting on the proper mounting of this exhibition?"

I wanted to clobber Alex Kepler right in the nose. "I have some clue," I said.

"Does *she*?" he asked. "Does she realize that without her, I can't even sneeze? My hands are tied by a twenty-three-year-old graduate student and I hardly need to tell you that I don't have time to stay here all spring waiting for her."

I took my suitcase out of the car and set it on the gravel, which gave me time to think, and time to silently thank Bailey for refusing to make the trip and keeping Alex waiting. "I'm sorry," I said, borrowing the words Bailey had said to me, "if handling my father's estate is such an inconvenience to you."

"It was your dad who demanded that we hang a show within a year of his death," Alex said. "I'm just trying to fulfill his wishes."

"And it was my dad who put Bailey in charge," I

said, "which is something we both have to live with." Had I been watching myself in a movie, I would have been flabbergasted to hear myself defending my father and the will that had caused me so much pain, but in the moment it felt entirely natural.

"Do you mind my asking what exactly is going on with her, Claire? I'm just trying to do my job here, and she's making it very difficult."

My first instinct was to say, *Yes, I do mind,* but then I realized I had some art world inside information; I could have some fun. "Well," I said, "at first it was that she was furious with me, but now it's that she's fallen in love—oh, and she just received an offer from David Geffen on one of the paintings from her thesis exhibition."

Alex squinched up the left side of his face in disbelief. "Are you kidding me?" he asked.

"About which part?" I said, taking great pleasure in drawing out the punch line.

He rolled his eyes. "David Geffen, of course."

"No," I said, "I'm not kidding."

"My God! What a story! The granddaughter of Paul Switzer selling a painting from her MFA show? It's extraordinary. What a stroke of genius Geffen's people had!"

"Actually, the painting is what's extraordinary," I said, stopping myself from adding, *you asshole.*

Alex cleared his throat. "Is there any possibility

Bailey might sign over her curatorial powers to you, seeing as she has so much else on her plate?"

I looked up toward the mountains, at the high peaks jutting into the blue sky. I thought of my dad, making his final trek up the chairlift, watching the trees glide by and the light on the snow, knowing that he wasn't going to see the spring that I now stood enjoying. How long had he spent writing his will? How many drafts had he written, how many trips had he made to the lawyer in the Diane von Furstenberg dress?

"Not a chance in hell," I said.

Alex led me into the study, where there were piles of folders, files, and albums on every horizontal surface. It looked like he had emptied out every closet, every flat file, every manila envelope in his quest for order. In front of the existing corkboard wall, three large bulletin boards on castors had been brought in, and each of these was plastered with thumbnails of photos. There were hundreds of thumbtacks, about the size of postage stamps, pinned in a grid. It looked like the plan for a very formal city of the future, where there would be no parks and rivers, just perfectly aligned streets.

"You've been busy," I said, and felt my attitude

toward Alex soften. He was, after all, here to do a job, and he was getting it done.

"Your dad had some ideas for this show," Alex said. "The organizing principle is to hang the works according to the time of day they were taken, so I've started by laying it all out—morning, noon, and night. But there are a lot of decisions to be made, and a lot of holes." He walked over to the board and pointed to a blank spot on the grid. "Here, for example, Paul mentions several shots taken within an hour of high noon, including *The Devil's Stepping-Stones*. There was one large-format image made, but there's no notation about the location of that original print. No one knows who has it. All Paul says about it is, 'Ask Bailey. Let Bailey decide.'"

"They were very close," I said. "She used to come up here in the summers and fish with him, and she would draw the fish and the lures. He thought she was a genius."

He nodded, as if this personal revelation from my life was not surprising in the least. "Sometimes it takes one to know one," he said.

I burst out laughing. *"Et tu, Brute?"* I asked, and when Alex looked at me, completely lost, I said, "Never mind. I'm sorry. It's a family joke."

Alex looked so wounded by my exclusionary comment that I felt compelled to say something nice.

"Look," I said, "I know we need Bailey, but until we have her, I can try to help locate the images you need." I picked up a black three-ring binder from the stack on the wooden counter. It had a large white typed label on the front: *Santo de Christo Mountains, December 1978.* Inside were plastic sleeves filled with slides that still looked crisp in their white plastic frames.

"The corresponding transparencies and prints are filed by date in the drawers under the windows," Alex said, clearly in his element now. "You'll notice that I have a set of symbols on each binder so we can instantly know how many other times he went to any given location and if any transparencies or prints were made from that specific trip."

"Smart," I said.

"In the case of somewhere like Moab, where he went repeatedly, the information is listed on a sheet of paper inside the front of each binder." He reached down to the floor and picked up a binder labeled *Moab, Utah, April 1983.* He opened the front cover and showed me the key.

"I was there with him once," I said, looking at his list. "In 1969."

Alex set down April 1983, and snatched another black binder off the floor. "That would be in here," he said, and I have to admit that I was impressed at his ability to pinpoint a time and a place.

I took the binder and flipped it open. There were the La Salle Mountains, the Kaibab Plateau, the red blazing sunsets. "I visited him in Moab when I was fifteen years old," I said. "It was hotter than Hades and I wanted to die."

"It must have been amazing to watch him choose his location," Alex said, "and to see how he measured the light."

"Not exactly," I said, flipping over the pages of slides, but before I could say how it could be boring and tiresome to watch him work, I flipped another page and stared in disbelief. On a sheet filled with slides of a brilliant desert sunset—piercingly beautiful reds washed over layers of rock and orange clouds slashed with pink—were three slides of a juniper tree on a rocky plateau. They were out of focus, off center, but there was no mistaking what they were.

"Oh my God," I said.

"Those seem as though they were taken with an older camera," Alex said. "Perhaps he was experimenting with a smaller format."

"No," I said, and looked up at him. "Where did you find these slides?"

He riffled through some notes. "Alone in a box in the closet. They're dated with his handwriting, just like the others."

I slipped the slides out of their protective sleeve and held one up to the light. There were the branches of the juniper tree framing the orange sky. There was the trunk I had focused on, all gray and gnarled. I could feel the heat of that sun on my skin, the way the rock scraped off the skin on my knee. "I took these pictures," I said. "On that trip when I was fifteen years old. These are mine."

Alex shifted his weight from one foot to another. He cleared his throat. "The dates appear to be in his handwriting," he said, reaching out a finger to point to the words on the plastic frame of the slide I held in my hand.

"That may be true," I said, holding up the three slides as if they were a royal flush and I'd just won the jackpot, "but I took these with my dad's old Nikon F. I've wanted to see the prints of these slides for almost forty years."

Alex cleared his throat again and stared at the floor. "Claire," he said, "you're not authorized to make prints of those slides."

I laughed and stared at him. "Are you kidding me?"

"No," he said, "I'm not. They're part of the bequest. Only Bailey is authorized to make prints."

I thought for a moment about bolting from the room—taking the slides, brushing past Alex, and making a dramatic escape to the photo-finishing store in Jackson—but instead I smiled, said, "Of course," and gently slid the three slides back into their protective cover.

It was Polly Jackson, girl of faith, who brought me back to the camera. In the summer of '75, just a few weeks after our graduation from college, she was marrying the son of a Boston banker at her father's church in Bar Harbor. No one had ever heard of Martha Stewart in 1975, but Polly didn't need coaching to pull off a picture-perfect wedding. The men would be in blue blazers and khakis. She would wear a pristine white cotton Laura Ashley gown. And the church would be festooned with white ribbon and pale pink roses. She asked if I would take the photographs.

"I don't even own a camera," I said.

"You can borrow my brother's," Polly offered.

"And then there's the matter of my not knowing how to use it."

"You have a degree in English from Bowdoin," she said. "I'm sure you can figure out how to use a camera."

It dawned on me a few days later why Polly thought I should be the one to line up the wedding party on the church steps and snap a picture of the first dance. She was a minister's daughter from a tourist town in Maine and she needed to pull out all the glitz she could for the Boston debutantes. I was the daughter of Paul Switzer. I would be there to add cachet.

I also know exactly why I consented to it. I still thought about those photos of the juniper tree that had never seen the light of day. I still wondered how they would have looked.

It was easy enough to get a camera. Everyone who had ever taken a photography course at Bar Harbor High School had used a Pentax K-1000. I myself had opted for home ec and woodshop, but my best friend, Laura Kern, had taken all three photography classes offered and went on to a high-profile career as our high-school yearbook photographer. I thought I could probably operate a K-1000 just from having heard Laura talk about it all those years. She used to go on endlessly about the camera and how fun it was to advance the film and focus the lens, and even though every one of her stories seemed to end in the darkroom with a chemical smell and a kiss, I think she really meant it; I think she really loved that camera.

A few weeks before the wedding, I went to pick up the K-1000 from Polly's brother Doug, who dug it out of his dresser drawer and made a big production out of blowing the dust off its steel case. He proceeded to show me how to advance the film and adjust the shutter speed as if he were a certified pro.

"I know, I know," I said, because I was so embarrassed that I didn't.

I ended up asking Mr. Moore, the guy at the drugstore, to help me load the film and to show me, again, how to adjust the settings, and once we had them set, I didn't touch the knobs and buttons until the day of the wedding. An hour before the ceremony was to start, I walked over to the rectory with the camera cradled in my arms like a baby.

"You nervous?" I asked Polly as her sister zipped up her dress—pure white cotton with an eyelet-framed square neck.

"I can barely breathe," she said, and then asked, "Are you?"

"Nervous?" I said. "Why should I be nervous? I'm not the one getting married."

"No," Polly teased, "but you're the one who has to make it look good."

The K-1000 was heavy, but somehow I didn't have to fight to hold it up. It fit in my hand. It felt good. When I pressed the shutter, and cranked the rewind button, the K-1000 felt like it came to life. It seemed to pull me where I needed to go—up or down, in or out—as if it possessed its own intelligence, as if it were working with me to get the shot. I focused on Polly and her banker, on the mother-in-law with her Chanel suit, on the bridesmaids in their pale pink dresses. When nothing else was happening—when the toasts went on too long, when the waiters were scrambling to get plates on the table—I took careful pictures of the lobster, the cake, and the tiny, sparkling bubbles of champagne.

"Hey, Claire," Doug Jackson said while I was in the middle of snapping a photo of a silver platter heaped with lobster. "Carol Miller wants to meet you."

"Who's Carol Miller."

"Groom's mother," he said, leading me across the room. We walked up to a table where the Millers sat with a group of perfectly coiffed friends.

"This is Claire Switzer," Doug said, "daughter of Paul."

Mr. and Mrs. Miller both stood and pumped my free hand. "We just adore your father's work," Mrs. Miller said.

"Really terrific stuff," Mr. Miller added.

"Thank you," I said. "He would be so honored to know it."

"In fact," Mr. Miller added, "we hope to see Yellowstone ourselves next fall."

"Really?" I said, as if no one had ever dared go to Yellowstone before.

"We have a little business to do out west," Mr. Miller explained, addressing his friends at the table. "And Carol, of course, has found a way to turn it into a vacation."

Everyone laughed and smiled at one another, pleased with Carol's cleverness.

"I'm sure you'll enjoy Wyoming," I said, and smiled. Before anyone could say anything in response, I lifted my camera. "I'd better get back to work," I said. "It was nice to meet you."

Later, after midnight, when I saw Doug sitting on a folding chair, I pulled up a chair and sat next to him.

"I love this camera," I said. "I want to buy it from you. Will you sell it to me?"

"If you want a camera, why don't you buy a new one?"

I shook my head. "I want this one," I said. "I'll give you fifty dollars."

"Candy from a baby," he said, but I still made him shake on it.

Mr. Moore, the man behind the counter at the drugstore, had white hair, red skin, and eyes that seemed too small for his face. When I went to pick up the developed pictures, he said, "You shot a lot of film," and smiled in a way that made it seem as if he'd found out something secret about me.

My heart pounded as I opened the glassine envelope to look at the negatives. What if they were blank? Off center? Blurry? Fuzzy? It was staggering how many things could go wrong. The memory of my ruined roll of film from Moab haunted me. I pulled out the first shot we'd staged on the church steps. Everyone's head was in the picture, and each head was smiling. The picture I'd taken of Polly as she walked out of the church and into the bright light of afternoon was beautiful. She was beaming, and you got the sense that she would never feel more at ease than she felt at that time and in that place. Best of all, however, were the pictures I'd taken of food. The red shell of the lobster looked like a ruby, and the cake—a four-tiered white cake with a buttercream basket-weave design topped with rosebuds—looked far better than it had in person. It had tasted like cardboard, but in my photo, it looked rich and light, as if one bite would taste exactly the way it felt to be in love.

"Can I get a couple extra copies of some of these?" I asked Mr. Moore. I had the impulse to put a photo of the cake in an album of my own. I could see it there, centered on a creamy-white page with nothing else around it. I could see it, in a black frame, hanging in the bakery where the cake had been created.

"Sure," he said, and while he wrote up the order, with his head still down and the redness of the part at the top of his head facing me, he said, "You did a nice job."

I would treasure those words for many years, taking them out, turning them around, and weighing them against the words my dad had never been able to say. When, more than two decades later, I began sending out my portfolio to see if being a photographer of food was something I could *be* rather than something I simply *did*, I could still hear Mr. Moore's compliment. My efforts to sell my work, however, were self-conscious and halfhearted. Unlike my dad, who met with a grand success the very first time he tried, it took me years and years of pounding on the gates before anyone bothered to open them—years of seeing postmarked envelopes in my mailbox, reading rejection letters, and agonizing over spending money on stamps; years of yearning and waiting and doubting—and even then, when the good news came, it wasn't a career-making sale. It was an offer to do an internship in the photo department at *Bon Appétit*.

"An internship?" I complained to Harrison. "At *my* age? I'm forty-four years old. I have a kid in high school. I couldn't possibly be someone's intern."

"Tell them who your dad is and they'll probably hire you."

"Not a chance."

"Because...?"

"If I'm going to do this, I'm going to earn it."

"Which is exactly the reason you need to be someone's intern."

When I got into bed the night after seeing my juniper-tree photos brought back from the dead, I closed my eyes, pulled up the covers, turned one way and then the other. A storm was brewing up the valley. The thunderheads had gathered at sundown, towering gray and threatening. A front. A wall. A wave that would crash down on us from Canada. One of my dad's most famous photos was of a buffalo in a thunderstorm. The animal was walking straight toward the viewer through a night that was murky, misty, hazy, wet. It looked like an apparition, like a giant creature coming out of the gloom with not entirely benign intentions. Its shoulders were enormous. Its fur was matted and wet. It looked like something that would be stalking this earth for another few millennia.

A print of that photo was hanging in the Wildlife Museum over the pass in Jackson Hole. It was hanging on the wall behind the landing of the main staircase leading down from the lobby to the galleries, so that every visitor to the museum confronted it just after making the commitment to descend to the galleries to see what there was to see of the animals of the West. It was impossible to walk toward that photo without stopping and catching your breath. I once stood at the railing above and watched three dozen people walk down the stairs—families with young children, women walking two by two, couples on dates, an elderly man all alone—and every single person stopped about ten or twelve steps before they got to the buffalo, and looked up, and breathed, and every single one of them made the decision to proceed closer to the animal, closer to their own idea of what being wild was all about, and they passed the photo with a kind of reverence. Every single one of them.

I threw back the covers, got up, and walked through the dark house to the study. Lightning flared through the sky in a flash of purple, its tentacles touching down over the Tetons. There were deer up there, moose, bear, backpackers. A deep rumble rolled through the valley, and it made me think of all the rocks that stayed in place year after year, hanging on to their place on earth even as the heavens tried to shake them off. There were rock slides and avalanches, of course, seasons of change, but the number of rocks that stayed in place was remarkable. There the mountains were, just as I'd seen them for the first time. There the river was, still making its way down the valley. I knew now that, although the shattered lens of a Nikon F looks awful, it's only a surface flaw. The film inside the camera I dropped would have been fine, and my dad would have known that when he told me, in his Jeep, that my pictures were gone for good. Why had he lied? And why had he kept them in his archives all this time?

I got out the three slides, put them into a small glassine envelope, and slipped them into my purse. I got back into bed, snuggled under the covers, and stared at the dark outside the window. The lightning kept flashing in rhythmic bursts as the storm moved down the valley. I counted the seconds until the roll of thunder, counted the minutes between the flashes of light. I stayed like that, eyes wide open, for several hours, until the only thing outside was the sound of rain.

CHAPTER FIFTEEN

The *next day,* Alex confronted me as soon as I walked into the study.

"Claire," he said, "I can't let you remove those slides from the collection. They're part of the bequest to the museum."

I smiled, marveling at how it was only yesterday that I had started to warm to Alex Kepler. Now he was back in his role as protector and defender of the estate, and he had identified me as a danger. I didn't mind, in a way. I was oddly calm and ready for the fight. "They're mine, Alex," I said coolly.

He shook his head quickly back and forth. "There's no proof of that."

"There doesn't have to be proof. I was *there*. I took them."

"I'm going to have to bring this up with our lawyers, and with Bailey."

"Fine," I said. "You can do whatever you need to do."

"And I'm going to have to insist that you leave them on the premises."

I glared at Alex. There was no way that, thirty-eight years later, some orange-haired man from a museum was going to deny me the pleasure of finally seeing those photographs. "You might remember that the premises you're referring to happen to be mine."

"I hardly think your father would have wanted his bequest compromised in this way," Alex said.

For most of my life, I would have claimed no authority over what my dad wanted. I didn't understand him, didn't share any kind of special connection with him, didn't really even *like* him. But at that moment I felt the fire of his blood flowing in my veins. "If I were you," I said, "I would be careful assuming you know anything whatsoever about what my father thought."

Alex bowed his head. "I'm sorry," he said. "You're right. I'm very sorry. Can we get back to work?"

We had to locate the whereabouts of the original print of *The Devil's Stepping-Stones*. No one could remember who had the photograph, and Alex thought there might be clues he had missed in the albums. If there were, I was no longer a good candidate for finding them; I was hardly paying any attention to what I was doing. I paged through albums from Alaska's Inside Passage, and a horse farm near Bozeman, Montana, that had originally been owned by the Harriman family of Western railroad fame, but all I could think about was myself at the time each photo was taken—how old I was, where I was living, what I was doing, and what part of my life my dad was missing. When I got to a series of photos taken in the Escalante Wilderness—slot canyons carved from limestone plateaus shot from above and below—I remembered a letter my dad had written to me about how dark the shadows were out there and how that matched his mood. A woman he had once loved—one of many, only the latest—had left him in Escalante, and he was sad and alone out there. My dad had been able to capture his despair with his camera—

contorted rock, black shadow. Even his worst days produced beautiful pictures. He couldn't, it seemed to me, do much wrong.

At six o'clock, the phone rang. It was Sam Penner, my dad's friend, the neurologist next door. "I saw a car in the driveway," he said. "I figured it was you."

"I'm working with the museum," I said, "trying to make sense of things."

"I bet Paul didn't make it easy for you, did he?"

"No," I said, "but you wouldn't expect that from him, would you, Sam?"

"No, I wouldn't," he said. "Can I bring over some dinner? I have a few buffalo burgers I was going to slap on the grill."

The thought of buffalo made me queasy, but I liked Sam. I always thought he was a good influence on my dad. I had hoped, in fact, that my dad would become more and more like Sam Penner as he aged—more mellow, less egocentric. I'd had no such luck.

When Sam arrived, we opened a bottle of Merlot from a case in the garage, cooked the burgers, and made salad from a head of overpriced organic lettuce that had probably been trucked all the way from South America.

"The word around town is that there's going to be a big show."

I nodded. "A retrospective," I said. "Every photographer's dream."

He looked at me. "Yours, too?"

I laughed. It was as if a comparison to my dad was on everyone's lips, just waiting for the tiniest provocation to be voiced. The only amazing thing was that Sam Penner hadn't actually used the word *genius*. "They don't do retrospectives of beer and chocolate so far as I know," I said.

"Neurologists don't get much public glory, either," Sam said, "but there's the private satisfaction, and I get this view for the rest of my life." He raised his glass to the Big Hole Mountains and the Grand Teton, lush and sun-kissed in the early-spring sun, jutting into the sky. "It's a nice prize."

Feeling emboldened by the wine and the comfortable presence of my dad's old friend, I waved my hand toward the dramatic skyline. "He would have snapped that view and made a photo people stand in line to see. Click. Done."

"You make it sound like a bad thing," Sam said.

I shrugged. "Not *bad*," I said, "but so damn lucky. He didn't have to live with doubt, or wrestle with the question of where his gift came from. He just looked and clicked and made magic like it was nothing."

Sam sipped his wine. "You didn't know your father

very well," he said quietly. It wasn't a condemnation or a challenge. He was merely stating a fact.

My mind raced to try to build a defense, but I found that I couldn't even conjure up an image of my dad's face, and I couldn't remember the name of the woman he lived with in Santa Fe when I was in high school, and although I could picture him eating trout for dinner, I couldn't remember what he liked to eat for breakfast. He was a genius, of course, an international figure in the world of photography, but I had only watched him work for a total of three weeks, and during most of those weeks, I'd had my nose in a book. I looked at Sam, frightened of what he might say next, but wanting to hear it all the same.

"He worked like a dog," Sam said.

I shook my head quickly—no. "He had amazing instincts," I said. "All his great photos came to him in a flash of inspiration. Hard work wasn't part of the equation. He wandered around to make a good show of things, I think, but he was just waiting for lightning to strike."

"Not true," Sam said, draining his glass. He was a very nice-looking man—one of those gray-haired men you see in magazines lounging on a sailboat wearing a watch with multiple time zones.

"Not *true?*" I asked, angry now at his presumption. "You've had too much to drink."

"My dear, the same could be said of you," he replied, and in response I poured myself more wine.

"Are those things in order by date?" Sam asked, indicating the albums.

"Oh, this guy Alex from the museum is meticulous," I said. "Not a shot out of order. I think I'm going to hire him to go through all my insurance papers next."

Sam laughed. He stood up, went over to the albums, and started to sort through them. He'd flip a page then stop and move to another album. Flip, then move. After about fifteen minutes, he came to a picture taken out on Owens Bridge, a single-lane little arc that crossed the Teton River about a half mile from the house. My dad had taken hundreds of pictures from that bridge. He liked the way the road curved in from the east, how the water narrowed between the rocks, how the grass blew in the wind in that spot. There is a picture in my front hall in Manhattan Beach of Bailey sitting on that bridge in summer shorts and T-shirt, her skinny legs dangling over the edge, her smile a gap-toothed image of glee.

"A few years after we met—the summer of '78, I think it was—I was fishing the Teton very early one morning," Sam said. "The caddis were hatching and the fish were going crazy. I'd been up since sunrise, walking up and down the shallows, having a ball. And I come around the bend and see your dad lying in the grass by the bridge, staring through his camera. Just lying there, staring. I waved, but he didn't put the camera down. I came over, but still he didn't put the camera down. Finally I said, 'Paul, you okay?'

" 'Fine,' he said, and that was that. I walked away, but soon after I had a nagging feeling that I'd seen something very peculiar—maybe a seizure or a ministroke. I went to look for him and found him back at the house. He looked like hell—eyes bloodshot, his face drawn. I don't think he'd eaten all day.

" 'What the hell were you doing out there?' I asked. And do you know what he said?"

I shook my head. I had no idea.

"He said, 'I was stalking a picture.' "

I rolled my eyes. "My dad expected things to come to him out of the clear blue sky, and they did. That was the thing with my dad. Everyone always said he was a genius, but you know what I think? I think he was just fucking lucky."

Sam put the album down. He walked across the room toward me, took the glass of wine out of my hand, and set it on the table next to the couch. Then he took my hands in his own, large ones—hands that at one time could have sliced into a brain, sewn a blood vessel, saved a life. I had never before felt my attention so completely seized by such a powerful authority, and I wanted to weep with the pleasure of it.

"Your dad's gone, Claire," Sam said softly. "Let him rest in peace."

I awoke at 3 A.M. in the tree bed with a headache hammering at my temples. I was still wearing my clothes. I rolled over and tried to remember when Sam had left. I remembered eating dinner, looking at the albums, drinking wine. I got up, got a glass of water and some Tylenol, got back into bed, and groaned when the bed felt as though it were a ship at sea.

I looked at the clock. It was 5 A.M. in Vermont. Harrison had presentations to give the next day, meetings, schmoozing underneath the maple trees with investors and financiers. I picked up my phone from the bedside table and called him.

"Hmm?" he asked.

"It's me."

"What's wrong?" he mumbled, and I realized that lately all I had offered Harrison was a serious of problems that needed to be solved, and all he had become for me was someone who solved them. That was the language of our marriage, the basis of exchange. When was the last time Harrison had asked for my help with anything? I hadn't helped him scout out a new pair of running shoes, hadn't helped him place a value on a hundred-year-old maple-sugar tree, hadn't helped him come to terms with the fact that our little girl was about to be gone for good. He hadn't asked, I hadn't offered. The same was true of our sex life. When was the last time I'd initiated anything? I hadn't greeted him at the door when he came home from work, unbuttoned his shirt, and kissed his neck; hadn't met him after a run to sit on the porch with a glass of water and make the suggestion that I could help him shower off the sweat; hadn't turned to him in the morning to touch him with a hand, a hip, a tongue. I accepted help from my husband, accepted comfort and pleasure, but I had been giving nothing in return.

"Nothing," I said. "I just wanted to say that I'm sorry."

"What time is it?"

I looked at the black curtains pulled around my bed, and at the blackness beyond them. I had come to know the patterns of the night in these mountains, the way the moon rose and fell in relation to the peaks, the way the sun broke over the valley. I knew it was 5 A.M., but what seemed important was that it well past midnight, not yet anywhere near dawn. "Morning," I said.

I heard him shift in his bed. He would be sleeping in a guest room on the second floor, the one with the brass headboard and the dormer windows that looked out at the pond and the barn and the woods. Out there, on the East Coast, the bright New England moon would have already ended its evening reign. "Sorry for what?" he asked.

"For being so flipped out about my dad and for all the stuff with work and for totally ignoring what's going on with you. You know what I realized this morning? I don't even know the names of the people you're selling the business to."

"It's okay," he said. "You've had a lot going on."

"No, it's not okay. I know what this company has meant to you and what it means for you to be giving it up. I should have paid more attention these past few months."

"I'm selling the business to a private equity firm whose principal partners are Rick Morales, Janice Waters, and Jamie Iriwan," he said.

"Are they nice?" I asked.

"They're sharks," he said.

"And they'll be there soon?"

"In a couple of hours. They got into Burlington late last night."

"You know what else I just realized?"

"What?"

"That it's been too long since I woke you up at dawn. I used to do that all that time, remember?"

"How could I forget?" Harrison said. "Those were the best days of my life."

"Are you serious?"

"Hell, yeah," he said. "I had a sexy new wife who couldn't keep her hands off me and a daughter on the way. Before I met you, I was just a dork—a guy running a business, spending every holiday at my sister's house and watching everyone else I know get married when I couldn't even find anyone I wanted to ask on a date. I thought I would end up old and alone in this very bed."

I pulled myself up on the fat pillows and pulled aside the curtains so that I could look out at the hulking shadows of the trees. "You are old and alone in that very bed," I said.

"Yeah—old, alone, and with a hard-on because my wife called with a sexy cross-country apology."

"That's all it takes to turn you on?" I asked. "You're that easy?"

"Always," Harrison said.

"I suppose I should apologize for that, too."

"I'd rather you just gave me a rain check for when we're back home."

"I can do that," I said, and then I took a deep breath.

"Did I ever tell you about the time I went out to Moab with my dad when I was a kid?"

"The time you broke his camera," he said, because he knew my life story. He carried it inside his head, side by side with his own.

"Yeah," I said, "and how he told me that the pictures I'd taken were lost for good?"

"Okay," Harrison said.

"I found the negatives. He kept them for nearly forty years."

"How do you know they're yours?" he asked.

"They're totally mine. I remember them exactly. Three shots of a juniper tree. I thought I was making great art."

"Did you?"

"Did I what?"

"Make great art?"

"No, they're blurry and off center and awful. But don't you see? He didn't keep them all this time because he thought they were good," I said, and with no warning, I got so choked up that I could barely breathe. When I spoke again, my voice came out like a kind of squeak or a cry. "He kept them," I said, "because they were mine." I took in a gulp of air, then squeezed my eyes shut and began to sob uncontrollably.

Harrison stayed on the other end of the line and

listened to me gasp and wheeze. There wasn't much he could do, after all, from two thousand miles away, other than to be present in my pain. When I was done, he said, "I'm sure your dad loved you very much, Claire. He just wasn't very good about showing it."

"I know," I said, and at that moment I wished desperately that my dad had not skied into a tree so that I could walk down the hall into his study, where he would be looking at images on film, or walk out to the river, where he would be fishing for trout, and tell him that I had loved him, too.

CHAPTER SIXTEEN

The *next morning,* after I nibbled on some toast, I walked down the road to Sam's house and knocked on his big wooden door.

"Up so early?" he asked.

"Can I ask you a question about my dad?"

"Of course."

"What was he stalking that day you saw him in 1978 on Owens Bridge?"

"I have no idea," Sam said.

"He started living with Caroline Greer that year."

Sam shrugged. "There were a lot of women in those days," he said. "I can't recall which came when."

"I can," I said. "Caroline Greer came shortly after my mother died. My dad gave me one of Caroline's rings the day of my mom's funeral. He did my mother the honor of putting on a tie and sitting in the church for the memorial service, and he gave me a piece of jewelry made by his new girlfriend. It was so touching."

Sam peered at me with eyes that had spent a life-time peering into the workings of people's minds. "I see her from time to time at the general store," he said. "Buying bread and huckleberry-raspberry shakes."

I understood that Sam was giving me something—an offering, a clue. "Thank you," I said, and turned to go.

"Claire?" he asked. I stopped, and looked back at him.

"He might not have been the best father," Sam said, "but he was a good man. And he loved you very much."

"Is that just something people say?" I asked. "Because it's the easy thing to say? 'He loved you, Claire.'"

Sam shook his head no. "The first time I came to your dad's house, he had *Morning Trout* on his wall," he said, "and I fell in love with it. I was just totally blown away by it. I offered to buy it on the spot, but he said it wasn't for sale. He said he thought he might loan it to a museum or a collector one day, but he never did. I kept asking if I could have it and he kept saying no, until one day—maybe ten years after I first saw it—he showed up with the thing on my doorstep and allowed me to hang it in my living room."

"I don't get your point," I said.

"You said he gave you that ring on the day of your mother's funeral," Sam said, "and I'm just saying that he didn't give gifts lightly."

I nodded, still totally perplexed, and then walked back to the house, climbed into the 4Runner, and drove slowly down the dirt road and into town.

My dad wasn't attracted by highly polished beauty. He always fell in love with women who loved the places he loved—the bush pilots, ski instructors, and local artisans who loved his small Western towns. There were probably a dozen women in the Teton Valley whom he had slept with or lived with or married, and I sometimes wondered if they ever got together to toast him or roast him or wonder what it was about him that they had found so attractive. I suppose if I had been a different kind of person, I could have tracked them all down, had them over for shots of whiskey. But I was, in the end, just me, and even asking after *one* of those women made it feel as if someone had opened a door and let in an icy blast of air.

I felt jittery as I walked into the general store, and stood there in front of the counter reading the menu of teas and milk shakes as if what I had come to do was find a remedy for my nerves.

"Can I help you?" a woman asked. She had a mass of curly brown hair pulled back into a bushy ponytail and eyes that made her look like a hawk. She was wearing a denim work shirt and a piece of polished jade on a leather strap.

"I'm Claire," I blurted. "Paul Switzer's daughter."

I don't know what I expected—for her to stare at me blankly and say, *So?* Spit on the counter and say, *Bastard!* Kindly ask what she could do for me? In any case, what she did do took me completely by surprise. She reached over the counter, took both my hands in hers, and said, "He was a good man."

I stood there for a moment, mesmerized by the warmth of her hands and the sympathy of her voice. Had she been my dad's girlfriend, a fellow artist, a neighbor, a friend? Part of me wanted to ask, but a larger part of me knew I needed to stay on task. I felt that I was close to something, though I had no idea what it was. "Thank you," I finally managed to say. "I wanted to ask if you know where I can find a woman named Caroline Greer. She's an artist. She makes jewelry."

The woman betrayed no surprise at my request.

"She lives over on the logging road. Her house is impossible to miss. Looks like a cross between a barn and a greenhouse."

"Wow," I said.

The woman raised her eyebrows in question, so I felt compelled to give an explanation. "I just didn't expect it to be so easy," I said.

She smiled. "Glad I could help."

The logging road ran alongside a cow pasture and took a sharp turn straight into the aspen trees. I drove slowly, watching for ruts and rocks and for the house I couldn't miss. I finally saw it, above the road to the left—a barn of weathered gray wood that looked as if someone had peeled off the top of the roof and one side and replaced it with thick panes of glass. I parked my car on the road and made my way along a path that had been stomped through the grass. I felt as if I were walking toward some kind of ice castle—an illusion that would melt as I approached— but the big front door was painted a cheerful red, and sitting on a small wooden table was a wrought-iron stand with a rooster on the top, and hanging from the stand was a bell with a string. I rang it, heard footsteps, and then Caroline was at the door.

She was a handsome woman—tall, with wavy auburn hair cropped close to her head, green eyes, and a delicate nose. She was wearing jeans, cowboy boots, and a knobby Irish fisherman's sweater that hung to her hips. There were silver rings on three of her fingers—a stack of thin rings that looked like interlocking waves; a band inlaid with turquoise; a think band etched with a tree—and around her neck on a silver chain hung a tiny glass labyrinth encasing a tiny silver bead.

"Caroline, it's Claire Brown," I said, in case she had forgotten what I looked like in the ten years since we last saw each other. "Paul Switzer's daughter."

"Of course," she said, and shook my hand. "How nice to see you again. I dreamed he was going to die, you know. But I didn't imagine the tree. The tree was brilliant, don't you think?"

I scrambled to keep up with the conversation. "It certainly worked, if that's what you mean," I said.

"It was swift, original, and above reproach," she said. "Which was what he always said he wanted."

"Original?" I asked.

"Well, a gunshot would have been such a cliché," she said. "Because it's so easy to get a gun in this town. The skiing accident lent the whole thing a satisfying air of sorrow."

"Death sort of lends itself to sorrow, doesn't it?"

"Not all deaths do," she said. "Would you like to come in? Have some tea?"

I followed her into the house, which was filled with a dazzling light. The high ceiling was crisscrossed by enormous whitewashed beams. There was a large round table surrounded by ten sturdy black Windsor chairs that looked so old they could have been the very chairs that the Founding Fathers sat in to sign the Declaration of Independence. High on the wall that had no windows hung three traditional ring quilts, and underneath them was a wrought-iron daybed fitted with a thick ticking-covered mattress and piled with more quilts and pillows. A hardcover book lay open on the mattress, and though I strained to see what it was, I couldn't make it out. Caroline led me to the kitchen, which was set against the wall of windows that faced the forest. There were a dozen bird feeders hanging in the trees outside, and birds seemed to be all around in the air, in the trees, on the ground. I sat on a bar stool and watched as Caroline set a pot of water on the stove and pinched fresh mint from a row of herbs that grew above her soapstone sink.

"Caroline," I said, "I'm trying to understand something about the summer of 1978." At the mention of the year, she didn't flinch or startle. She continued to get down mugs, fill the teapot, and fish tea bags out of an earthenware crock on the counter, so I forged ahead with the question I'd come to ask. "I wanted to ask what you know about a technique my dad used. I believe he called it 'stalking.'"

"Of pictures or women?" she asked, without missing a beat.

"Pictures," I said, and I pressed my tongue to the top of my mouth to keep myself from blurting out anything more.

Caroline turned to face me. "It was a technique he would use when he felt like he couldn't see," she said.

I felt the ground roll. It took me a few moments to remember that I was sitting in a glacier-carved valley on the Western divide and not on an earthquake fault at the edge of a continent. It had only been my knees buckling; it had only been my mind that lurched. *"He felt like he couldn't see?"* I repeated, hitting hard on each word to make sure I got it exactly right.

"Yes," she said, matter-of-factly. "He couldn't see the underlying geometry of nature. He became disconnected from the source of his talent. So I suggested that he take a picture a day for three straight months. Just one picture and no more than one. It took his mind out of the process and forced him to trust his unconscious again. Stalking was what we called it because he loved that sense of being on the hunt and the whole notion that there were good pictures out there as long as he paid close enough attention."

"Sounds like Thoreau with a thirty-five-millimeter."

She shrugged. "It was, in way. It was a technique I learned from watching birds choose the things they use to make their nests. If you watch carefully, you'll see that they don't just pick sticks at random. They pay very close attention to color, to thickness, to length. They're very deliberate, but in a very organic way. Birds don't stress about building their nests; they just do it."

"Do you know if any of these photos survived?"

She peered at me, sizing me up in exactly the way that it seemed Sam had done earlier in the day.

"What if I told you that I just wanted to see them for personal reasons?" I asked.

"I might not think you were telling the truth," she said. "Because you and your dad didn't have a very personal relationship. You didn't seem to get along very well, at least not from my perspective."

I looked her straight in the eye. "No," I said, "we didn't get along very well. We didn't understand each other very well. I'm trying to change that."

She slid a mug of tea across her butcher-block counter. "It's a little late for that, don't you think?"

"Actually, yes," I said. "But I don't have a lot of other options."

She took a sip of her tea, and before she had raised her head, she said, "Would you like to see some negatives?"

I set my own mug carefully on the counter. "You have *negatives*?"

She went to a tall red armoire, took out a plastic sleeve and an old-fashioned light box—the slanted kind with a lightbulb underneath the white plastic. She plugged it in, and set the sleeve onto the light. It was a series of film taken over the course of a month in the spring of 1978. On the bottom of each piece of film, a date had been written in small black ballpoint pen. There was an image dated April 3 of the moon on a night when the moon had little to say. It was an unremarkable picture of an unremarkable night sky and all I could think about were the pictures he didn't choose to take that day. There must have been so many decisions, so many near misses, so many times when he looked and assessed and saw and decided: *no, not that one, something better will come if only I wait.*

The next day, there was a picture of a fox staring through the brush, but its face was obscured in a way that was distracting, not mysterious.

On April 5, there were wet rocks on a shoreline.

On April 6, leaves floating on the water like a flotilla of aimless boats. The images went on like this for two weeks—some of them good, some of them bad, all of them unremarkable—and then on April 19, there was a flock of birds perched on a telephone wire like musical notes on a staff, but there was something to it—a rhythm, a purpose. I could feel that something had shifted, but then the series ended.

"I don't get it," I said. "What happened on April twentieth?"

"On April twentieth, we hiked up to the Devil's Stepping-Stones. It was one of those crystalline days, with wildflowers in full bloom up near the tree line— well, you know what it looked like. Everyone knows what it looked like."

The shot he'd taken that day was one of his most iconic. It had run as a spread in *National Geographic:* an alpine field of wildflowers below the snowcapped peaks of the Grand Teton set against a big blue sky. It had been made into postcards and posters that you could still buy in the tourist shops in Jackson Hole.

"You have it, then, the original image?"

She pointed at the wall behind me. I turned, and saw the missing photograph hanging there beside the front door I had walked through only a few moments before, preserved between sheets of archival glass and framed in polished ebony.

"He gave it to you?" I asked, remembering what Sam had just told me about how my dad never gave gifts lightly.

"For safekeeping," she said. She walked over to the photograph. She gingerly lifted it off the wall and set it on the ground.

On the back, in pencil, in my dad's odd left-leaning scrawl, were these words: *Devil's Stepping-Stones, Targhee National Forest, April 19, 1978.* Underneath the line of writing, some words had been erased. You could see their smoky smudges, the faint outline of an *e*, the tail of a letter that might have been a *g* or a *y*.

"What was erased?"

She went back to the drawer where she had kept the negatives. She pulled out an envelope and handed it to me. Inside was a photograph of the words we were looking at on a day when they were still whole. Below the identification line, my dad had written: *First fruits of stalking. Thanks to Caroline.*

I looked up. "He decided to *hide* it?"

"His taking pictures in this way was a very private exercise," she said. "He didn't want people to know. He became very good at giving the appearance of improvisation," she said, "but from the time I knew him, anyway, his photographs were for the most part intensely worked out."

"He destroyed thousands of negatives before he died. Did he forget you had these?"

She nodded. "I believe he did. I have several series. I love them more than the work that made him famous."

I felt dizzy. I'd had an entire life figured wrong.

With digital photography, you end up with a natural, irrefutable series of images. Shooting large-format film, however, yields a pile of individual pieces of film. You slide each piece of film into the camera, take your shot, and slide it out. There is no way to ensure that any given image was taken before or after any other given image unless someone has been paying careful attention, and if that someone had recorded dates and times on the negatives. Caroline Greer could have manufactured the series of images she showed me. She could have cobbled them together to make up a story. But I knew without a doubt that what she had shown me was the truth about my dad that I had been seeking my entire life; I couldn't wait to try it for myself.

I drove straight from Caroline's house over the pass to Jackson. There was a camera shop on the edge of town. I parked, walked in, went up to the counter, and said, "I'd like a camera."

The guy at the counter was younger than me, with dark hair and an air of relaxed smugness about him.

"Point and shoot?" he asked.

"No," I said, scanning the shelves behind him. "Can I look at the Nikon D300?"

"That's twelve-point-three megapixels," he said, turning to get the camera. "It'll run you a couple thousand."

I took the camera from his hands, lifted it, looked through the lens. It had a nice feel in my hands and a pleasing weight. My fingers instinctively found the dials and buttons and slides I would need to frame a good shot. "I'd like to see the AF-S Nikkor fourteen to twenty-four mm," I said, pointing to an ultra-wide-angle lens that I knew would cost more than the camera itself.

The camera guy raised his eyebrows, pulled out the lens, and handed it to me without saying a word. I fitted the lens on the camera body, fiddled with it, looked, focused.

"May I see the seventy to two hundred mm?" I asked. He brought down the zoom lens, and then before I could form the thought, he brought out a sleek black Tamrac backpack that would house the expensive gear.

"I'll take it all," I said, and slapped down my credit card. "Oh, and one more thing..." I fished the glassine envelope out of my purse and slid it across the counter. "Could you please make a set of prints from these slides?"

I went next door to a souvenir shop and bought

a postcard of my dad's famous shot of the Devil's Stepping-Stones. The words *Beautiful Jackson Hole* were written across the top corner with a flourish in gold. I wondered how many people had purchased that photo who knew that it was, actually, taken in Idaho. I wondered how many people believed that he had snapped it, without preparation or planning, just like Ansel Adams and the Mexican graveyard.

Later that evening, I walked down to Owens Bridge as the sun was going down. I watched as the pink glow washed over the water, as it turned pale and then blue. I held my new camera poised the entire time to snap a photo, but how could I decide whether or not the pink would get any clearer? How could I know that the blue wouldn't give way to a luminous gray? The moment never came, but I felt myself yearn for it as if the yearning were a tangible thing.

The next morning, I called Michelle Dorsey, the cupcake editor. "I'm going to have to cancel," I said.

"Cancel what?"

"The whole project. I can't do it."

She laughed, but when I didn't laugh with her, she said, "The whole *project*?"

"I'm sorry," I said. "My father recently died. There's some business I need to take care of."

After I hung up, I pulled on my hiking boots, packed a day pack with water and lunch, grabbed my camera, and drove up to the Grand Targhee National Forest. It's about an hour away from Dad's house to the north. You drive to the trailhead along the bottom of a canyon where the Lower Teton River empties out in a wide flat plain carved by an ancient glacier. The rise is gradual. I parked in a lot that was very nearly full and began to walk through the fern-lined path. I snaked back and forth across the rushing stream and through fields choked with bluebonnets. I passed a family splashing in one of the snowmelt pools, some Japanese tourists who were posing for a snapshot on one of the bridges, and I was passed by a group of three college boys who explained that they were trying to make Tapeat's Peak by sunset and had gotten a late start. After about an hour and a half, the trail began to climb over a series of shelves, and the canyon began to narrow. Rock outcroppings appeared along the trail. The peaks of the lower Tetons began to pierce the sky. After two hours, I came over the crest of a rise, and there it was: the view my dad had made famous.

I sat down on a boulder and took out the postcard. I looked around for higher ground, because it appeared that he had stood higher than even a tripod would allow. There was a large outcropping of rock to my right, so I packed up my gear and waded into the flowers. Bees scattered, pollen flew. I held my camera in my hands above my head as if contact with so many flowers would be as damaging as water. I clambered up on the rocks, then hoisted myself up even higher. I squatted. I sat. Then I decided that he must have been at the next outcropping. I climbed down, waded back to the trail, waded to the next group of rocks, climbed up. When I was satisfied I had the right spot, I got out my camera and considered the light.

My heart was pounding. I had just one shot. Could I capture the same glory my dad had captured under the exact same circumstances? The year of his photo had been wet like this one and the flowers were thick. He had climbed the same path, he had waded through flowers that were ancestors of the ones I had waded through today. He'd had a clearer sky, more perfectly formed marshmallow clouds. But the sky was still there, blue and thin; the clouds were still there, white and scattered.

I fiddled with the camera settings, then lifted it and looked through the lens.

I heard laughter coming from the trail. I lowered my camera and waited for the hikers to pass. They saw me when they rounded a bend and waved. I waved back. There were two of them, two men, both with cameras slung around their necks. One of them had a serious telephoto, which could capture the veins on the wings of a bee or the whorls of moss on a rock. As the men got closer, the one with the lens called out, "Classic shot you've got there."

"Looks like you may have gotten a few of those yourself today," I said, nodding at his camera. He stopped walking and his friend stopped beside him.

"We'll see," he said. "Light's a bit weak." The friend swung off his day pack and got out a water bottle. "What are you shooting with there?"

"A Nikon D3."

The man whistled. "Nice," he said. "And you've got the iconic location there, too."

I laughed—a short, sharp burst of sound that wasn't at all the sound of amusement. The friend had capped his water bottle, swung on his pack. The pair was preparing to leave, and something about the clear, high mountain air, something about the absurd coincidence that someone who could identify what I was doing had happened to walk by, compelled me to open my mouth.

"Paul Switzer was my dad," I said.

The man with the lens looked at me. "No shit?" he said.

I shrugged, spread out my arms and my hands as if to say, *I'm just speaking the truth.*

The man turned to his buddy. "You hear that?" he asked. "She's Paul Switzer's daughter."

"Are you a photographer, too, then?" the friend asked.

I felt light-headed, dizzy, glad I was sitting. I could have said, *Yes I'm a photographer but not quite as brilliant.* Or, *Yes I'm a photographer but not quite as visionary.* There were so many ways to answer that question and none of them seemed like the truth because the truth was that I didn't have the slightest idea what I was. I was someone who took pictures that were painstakingly stage-directed, but wasn't that the same thing my dad did when he hunted down a shot? I was someone who made her living with a camera in her hands, but I did so at the request of corporations bent on making money and it didn't seem at all the same thing as what my dad did when he went out looking for beauty. I was someone who had, of late, not been able to believe that I could still do it, that I had ever been able to do it, that there was any reason for me to keep trying it at all because there was another genius in my family, another seer, another sage. So what did that make me?

"Yes," I finally said, "I am."

After they left, I held my finger poised above the

button until my arm started to shake. I finally pushed the shutter with my eyes closed, as if I were praying—and when I opened them, I saw the gorgeous scene in front of me—the flowers and the rock, the trees and the sky, and I couldn't wait to get back to my studio in L.A. to see if I had captured the essence of it.

When I got back to my dad's house, I told Alex that I had an idea for the exhibition.

He shifted his weight from one foot to the other. "Look, I don't know everything that's going on with you and Bailey," he said, "but I know about Paul Switzer's will, and frankly, I don't think it's your right to be making those kinds of decisions."

"Of course I would run it by Bailey, Alex, just like you'll be doing with your ideas."

"Okay," he said. "What is it?"

"It would be a way to show how he worked," I said. "To show that the appearance of improvisation he cultivated was actually the result of design. We could show a series of daily studies he took that led up to one of the iconic images. It would be a way to cap off the exhibition, a kind of exclamation point."

Alex looked at me. His eyes looked tired. "My

research indicates that your dad didn't work that way," he said. "And all his writings and teachings—"

"I know," I said. "I know. That's the public image of Paul Switzer, but the private reality was something else. I know because I think I saw him doing it when I was twelve years old, and other people saw him do it, too. It's why he destroyed so many negatives—not to raise their value but to hide his process."

Alex seemed surprised. He seemed ready to become excited. "Do you have proof of this?" he asked.

"Maybe," I said.

"If you can produce negatives or images, it would be an important discovery, Claire."

"I can try," I said.

Alex looked directly at me. "But your time may be better spent producing Bailey, at this point."

CHAPTER SEVENTEEN

The next day, I went back to Caroline's house, and she opened the red door as if she was expecting me.

"Will you allow *The Devil's Stepping-Stones* to hang in the exhibition?"

She shook her head. "I'm sorry," she said. "He gave it to me for safekeeping." She didn't move, but it was as if, with her words, she'd taken a step between me and the treasure that was inside her house.

"You kept it safe for twenty-eight years while he

was alive," I said. "Perhaps it doesn't need safekeeping anymore."

"That photograph has been reproduced so many times for so many purposes," she said, "and I'd like to protect the integrity of the real thing. I think that was his intention."

"What about the negatives?"

Caroline threw back her head and laughed. I could see a gold tooth in her mouth, the dark cave of her throat. "No," she said, when she caught her breath, "not those."

"They show the way he worked, they show that he was mortal. Bringing them to the public's attention would heighten people's awareness of him. There would be arguments, theories, new studies of his work. I mean, these negatives would make headlines. They would be big news. Someone who worked so hard to plan his death and retrospective would love all that attention, don't you think?"

"He hated the idea of mortality. He'll make headlines in his own way."

"So you're going to protect him? His false reputation as this man who just tossed off his best shots?"

She looked at the woods behind me—at the birds and their houses and the trees and their shadows. "Yes," she said, "I am."

I took a step back, as if preparing to go. "Why would you do that?" I asked. "He left you. He stopped loving you. He pulled his entire estate away from you."

"People like Paul live by their own rules. That's what makes them great. He loved me very well while he was loving me."

On the flight back to Los Angeles, I held my Nikon in my lap. Everything around me begged to be made into a photograph. There was a little girl in the seat in front of me who kept peeking at me with huge green eyes and a freckled nose. There were fibers on the carpet on the floor of the airplane that looked like tumbleweeds. I saw magic in the bubbles of my Diet Coke, which the flight attendant had poured so expertly into a plastic cup. I could take a picture of the clouds out the window, the Grand Canyon gaping below us, the crush of passengers waiting to step off the airplane, the taxi driver with his deep, dark skin and his wary, black eyes.

When I walked into the house, Harrison was lying on the big leather sofa just inside the front door. He was stretched out full length, eyes closed, tie loose. The curtains were drawn and a half-empty bottle of champagne stood on the table next to two empty glasses, one of them used, one of them dry, the cork and the foil nearby—a perfect tableau for a photo. He sat up when he heard me.

"We closed the deal this morning," he said. "They gave me everything I wanted." He grabbed the champagne. "Can I pour you a glass?"

I stepped forward, wrapped my arms around his neck, and kissed him hard on the mouth. His skin was scratchy, his eyes were bloodshot, and there was a roughness in the way he kissed me back. "That sounds good," I said, "and you feel good. Congratulations." I expected that we would fall into the intimacy we'd shared over the phone, but Harrison abruptly pulled back from me and turned toward the champagne. "It's a dubious honor," he said bitterly, "selling out."

I reached over and rubbed his shoulder. "You'll be able to invest in other young companies," I said. "You'll be able to keep the spirit of entrepreneurs alive. Your great-grandfather would have loved that."

"My great-grandfather loved making maple syrup," he said, handing me a glass of champagne. I took the glass, sipped, and watched while Harrison refilled his own glass and drained it. "So were you going to tell me that you backed out of the cookbook project?" he asked. "Or did you think it would be somehow amusing to have Michelle Dorsey call me and break it to me herself?"

"Oh my God," I said. "I meant to tell you. I swear I did, Harrison. I'm so sorry."

"You made me look like a fucking idiot."

"I totally forgot," I said. "I just totally forgot because I discovered something important about my dad."

"What?" he said flatly. I had pushed him to the edge of something—to some line, some horizon. I hoped my story would bring him back.

"I went to see Caroline Greer," I said, "and she has a bunch of negatives. They prove that my dad worked his butt off to get his big shots. He had this system, this process. He would take the entire day to track down a good image, and only gave himself one chance to take it—one piece of film per day. It forced him to see things in a completely new way. It forced him to push through his doubt and despair, and what he found were his best shots. *The Devil's Stepping-Stone, Buffalo Morning, Midnight Arches*—they were all taken this way."

Harrison flopped down on the couch and considered what I was saying. I imagined raising my camera and taking a picture of his tie, which was a blue Robert Talbot with an intricate geometric print, hanging loose and discarded around his neck. "No one knows about this?" he asked.

"Caroline Greer, Sam Penner. I'm guessing Bailey knows, and you and me."

"And you're sure this is real?"

"Dead sure. And Harrison? I tried it myself. That's why I can't shoot cupcakes right now. I have to try it for myself."

"A picture a day."

"Exactly. As a way of trying to see again. It's like Thoreau going into the woods, stripping things back, getting to the essence of things."

"What did you take a picture of today?"

"I haven't yet. That's the thing. It's completely agonizing. Pictures form before your eyes, and you have to choose. You have to risk. You have to *see*."

"You could have told me," he said. "We could have rescheduled the cookbook."

"I'm sorry," I said. "I can't take pictures of cupcakes right now. I just can't."

"Well, can you go to the game tonight? Lakers versus Mavericks. Bailey went over to get Tommy. They'll be back in half an hour." Just like that, he had forgiven me.

I shook my head. "I want to download my photos."

He grabbed my hand and pulled me down on top of him. He kissed my ear, my neck, my breast through my clothes. "Sometimes you really piss me off," he said.

I thought about pulling back, walking away and stewing in guilt and remorse as I stalked the day's photo, but I remembered the promise I had made to Harrison over the phone the other morning—a promise to be more open to him—so I sat up on top of his hips, pulled my shirt over my head, and whispered, "Do I?"

Harrison, Bailey, and Tommy ended up going to the game without me. The moment they were gone, I slipped outside and walked back to the studio. The fog had reduced the beach to a string of streetlamps, like fuzzy yellow planets. I hadn't taken a picture yet today; I'd passed them all by, perhaps to make room for this one moody piece. I swung my camera up to my eye, framed the bright halos, and clicked.

I flipped on the lights in the studio, punched on my computer, and while I waited for it to boot up, I walked back to Bailey's room. She had started a new painting for the dealer who would be giving her a solo show. It was the face of a man, filling nearly the entire canvas. She was forming the features of the face with fractured pieces of painted paper. His hair was wild and blond, springing off the surface of the canvas in layers of metallic gold. He gazed out at the viewer like a modern-day David, like some kind of god.

It's a powerful thing to watch a painting come to life

over time. You can do it now, without any investment, on Web sites devoted to showing painting happening in real time, but watching a person paint in real life has a whole different flavor. Paint has dimension, for one thing. It sits on the canvas lightly or heavily, it fills in the ridges or plasters over them, it builds up in waves and valleys. Oil paint has a distinctive smell, as well—the smell of chemistry, of industry, of potential explosions. It sickens some people, but for others it is the smell of possibility, of beauty, of life.

The whole reason we pay any attention to art or artists is that it gives us a way to get into someone else's head. We ask a painter, "What was your inspiration? What techniques did you use? Why did you choose to put this line there?" but what we really want to know is, "What's inside your head? What's it like in there?" Looking at Bailey's painting of Tommy emerge in the room at the back of my studio was like watching a master class in confidence. She would stroke an orange-tinged yellow on his mouth and then just as assuredly the next day turn it to red. Things would build around and over it—layers of green, purple shadows, the black in the hollows beneath his eyes—and for a while you would think that the orange tinge was gone. But in the end, that color would still be there—the smallest wisp of it, the perfect counterpoint. It took my breath away.

I closed the door and went back to my desk to download my two photos—my own version of the Devil's Stepping-Stones and the streetlights on the beach in Manhattan. I opened up the mountain photo first, and held my breath while it came in, one line of pixels at a time, as if it were emerging from the mist. I exhaled. It was a good photograph—solid composition, crisp lighting, and beautiful scenery—but it was nothing like my dad's photo. I reached into the pocket of my jeans and pulled out the crumpled postcard. I propped it up beside the screen. Even though it was small and printed on high-gloss paper, it was dazzling. It made you feel as if you were standing right there in the field of flowers, as if that brilliant sky was stretched out overhead. It made you feel as if you were standing in the presence of something divine. Mine didn't. And it was the same thing with the moody beach scene. I'd taken a nice photograph, but the dark wasn't dark enough, the lights weren't bright enough, the halos didn't translate in a way that would make people stop and stare and think and reflect.

I was careful to leave the photo files on my camera instead of transferring them to my computer, where any one of my staff or my family could see them. The computer was too public a place to keep such private musings. I shut everything down and went to sleep.

* * *

That night, I dreamed about a tsunami just like the one from 2003's tragic headlines. There was a wall of water forming out at sea, gathering speed and power, racing toward our house while we slept, and though we'd called ourselves lucky to live on the beach, though we'd been so pleased to live far from the slickness of Hollywood and the frenetic pace of New York, it would be our life on the beach that finally brought about our deaths. I awoke abruptly in a cold sweat. My heart was beating wildly, and I lay there until it fell into the cadence of the waves. Then I lay there listening to the silence of the house. I heard a car door slam sometime later, but I remained curled up on my side of the bed, pretending to be asleep.

When I awoke the next morning, I left Harrison sleeping in bed beside me. I crept down the hall to Bailey's room, and could see her sleeping, too. Downstairs, I had a cup of tea, and then went to the studio to look, again, at my two photos and analyze what I had done wrong and how I could do better today. Could I frame things differently? Choose a different way to handle the light? When I stepped through the French doors, however, I felt something foreign in the air, something strange. It felt, at first, like something dangerous. I looked down the hall and saw that the door to Bailey's room was open. I had left it closed the night before.

I walked down to her room and looked inside. Tommy St. John was asleep on the couch. I stood there for a moment trying to reconcile the image: Bailey's boyfriend asleep on the couch in her studio. Had they slept together on that couch? Had she refused to let him in the house? As fast as the questions came to me, a logical story followed: Of course Bailey and Tommy were sleeping together. Any fool could see that. This man, sprawled out before me, was my daughter's lover. I squeezed my eyes shut, but when I opened them, I couldn't pull myself away from the sight of Tommy sleeping in the place where I had seen Bailey sleeping just days before.

He was wearing a faded blue T-shirt and jeans. One lean, muscular hand rested on his chest and the other was stretched above his head. His face was in complete repose and his hair, which fanned out around it—that extraordinary corkscrew hair—looked exactly like a halo. I looked at the portrait of Tommy on the easel, looked at Tommy himself on the couch, then back at the easel.

I'm not the kind of person who would travel to somewhere like Calcutta or Cameroon and find local, colorful people—usually poor, usually destitute—and snap their photos. I could never do it. I couldn't have taken the famous photo of the naked Vietnamese girl running from napalm. Even if I later got permission, a signature, some sense of acceptance from the subject, I would feel as if I had taken something that wasn't mine. I knew that what I was doing that day was wrong. I could see its wrongness as if I were a member of a jury carefully weighing the facts of the case: a mother, a daughter, a camera, a boyfriend. It would be wrong to take this photograph. But my heart was beating with the thrill of the hunt. I had found today's subject—an image that would be sparkling and clear, that would show something larger than what can be shown with a bar of chocolate or a tomato just plucked from the vine. I took a deep breath, raised my camera, and pushed the shutter.

Most people can sense when a photographer is present. There's something about being watched that makes the air vibrate at a different frequency. Tommy opened his eyes, tilted his head, and saw me standing in the doorway with the camera.

He blinked. "What's going on?" he asked.

"Nothing," I said, backing out. "Sorry to bother you."

*   *   *

People say that digital technology has taken away the soul of photography, but I find that the soul of it is largely unchanged. The camera is still a piece of equipment you hold in your hands and the photograph is still a thing that captures light. From the beginning of photographic time, people have stood and waited to see what it was that they saw through the lens, to compare what they remember they saw to what can be perceived directly in front of them. You used to stand in a darkroom, with the sharp smell of ammonia-like chemicals wafting around you, a dark so complete it takes the whole world away, and you wait, and watch, as the image swims to life over the course of hours, days, or even a week. So, too, you now stand in front of a computer, with the hum of electronics and the vaguely blue light all around, and wait for the pixels to sparkle to life. The gratification is instant, but the process is the same.

The shot of Tommy asleep in front of his portrait had something to it. There was so much to look at— Tommy's extraordinary hair appearing once on his head and again on the canvas behind him, alive with Bailey's magic; the man asleep and the portrait unfinished. There was a message in my photograph about the nature of creativity and art and inspiration. There was a point being made, a stance being taken, and I was the one who was taking it. I couldn't wait until the next day when I'd have the chance to take another picture.

But later that day, Bailey came storming into the kitchen, where I was setting out the enchiladas that Marisol had left us for dinner.

"Did you take a picture of Tommy?" she asked, with venom in her voice. We had come to a peaceful détente over the incident with the painting, but there was poison between us again. I had stepped over the line, and once again I felt the sting of my mistake. What defense could I possibly give for taking the photo of Tommy? What could I possibly say that Bailey would understand? My mouth opened and closed, but nothing came out.

"Did you?" she demanded, stomping her foot like a belligerent toddler. "Because that's the weirdest, creepiest thing I've heard in my entire life. He's my *boyfriend*, Mom. Why do you want a picture of him? Why are you even *looking* at him?"

I wanted to say, *Please, no, not again.* I wanted to run from the room and cry. I wanted to put my hands on her shoulders and say, *Calm down.* "I'm doing a study," I said, as simply as I could.

"A study of my *boyfriend*?" she shrieked. "*Of my boyfriend*?"

"No, Bailey," I said, willing myself not to fly apart. "A study in how to see. I'm taking a picture a day. Tommy was asleep on the couch in front of the portrait you're making, and it was a great composition. I thought it would make a good picture."

She shook her head, spun around so that her back was toward me, then spun back again. "You thought it would make a good *picture*?" she demanded.

"I think I figured something out about my own work," I said. "I found these negatives in Grandpa's study that I took when I was twelve years old, and I'm trying to go back and, I don't know. Learn how to see."

Something in the air changed. The molecules moved around, fused together, and became something solid between us. The air grew cold.

"Don't take any more pictures of my boyfriend," she said. "And don't come anywhere near my art. And if you take anything out of Grandpa's study, I swear to God I'll take you to court."

CHAPTER EIGHTEEN

The next day the crew came from *Art Forum* to interview Bailey and take her picture. I felt as if I were being physically assaulted when another photographer scouted my house to look for the best light, set up flags on C-stands, measured the depth of field, and focused his camera on my daughter. How many thousands of pictures of her had I taken over the years at school events, and cross-country races, holidays, and Sunday evenings when the light at the beach at sunset was shocking pink? I wanted to scream, I wanted to yell, I wanted to take the photographer's camera and fling it to the floor. Instead, I crept around the edges of the action, pretending not to care while my eyes and ears strained to take in every detail. I lurked in the shadows, stood behind doors, opened a window on the second story in order to capture the sound.

"That's nice," the photographer said. "Hold it. Smile. Good."

The interviewer was a young guy named Chris. He had a shaved head and large, black, square-framed glasses that reminded me of a 1950s news anchor. He perched on the edge of our couch as if it might swallow him whole if he dared sit back. "So," he said, "how does it feel to stand at center of the white-hot art market?"

Bailey laughed—a delighted, gleeful trill that proved she already knew how to occupy her fame. She was already at peace with the fact that she would be a working artist, while other people her age would have to wait tables or become nannies in order to secure their place in the world. Had it been me, I might have protested at the notion of anything happening overnight, and then hammered away at how hard I had worked, and for how long. I might have talked about my artistic pedigree and how the granddaughters of famous artists who want to make art have to earn their own way, perhaps more than the granddaughters of other men. "It feels fantastic," she said.

"*Winter Wave* both resembles your current work and seems to be a leap forward toward something new. Do you credit Art Center with this kind of growth?"

"Art Center gave me the time and space to find my own creative voice," Bailey said. "It gave me the technical training I need to pursue my craft. *Winter Wave* was actually created in one night, but it was a night that wouldn't have been possible without the work I did at Art Center these past three years."

Chris scribbled. "One night?" he said. "Tell me more."

She shrugged, and then tossed out a perfect sound bite. "The best art is always an emergency."

"That's good," Chris said. "That's very good."

"It's the only possible response to the given moment. It's the only thing you can do."

"And the emergency for this painting was ...?"

I held my breath while I waited to be exposed—*my meddlesome mother, my pathetic mother, my boundarybreaking mother*—but before I could exhale, Bailey gave her answer. "The emergency," she said, "was my grandfather's death."

Chris nodded and pushed his pen across the page.

"I learned everything from my grandfather," Bailey explained. "He taught me about light and composition and the movement of clouds. He taught me about the importance of instinct and the power of creativity. Above all else, he taught me to honor my own vision and not to accept anyone else's version of what makes good art. His death has been a terrible loss, but his life has been an inspiration to me. The emergency was simply that he's now gone, but I'm still here."

Chris looked up. "Do you believe there is an art gene?" he asked. "Can the ability to make art be passed on from one person to another?"

I leaned forward, straining to hear every word.

"I believe that our DNA loads the gun," Bailey said, "and our environment pulls the trigger. If you're the son of, say, a baseball great, you have some essential baseball wisdom inside you that allows you to hear the rhythms of the game. The same thing is true of artists. Something was inside me that primed me to be able to see color and shape and line the way I do; I know that for a fact. But my grandfather taught that part of me to reach out and touch the canvas."

For my photo that day, I ended up taking a picture of

the photographer's camera, which he had set down on the limestone countertop of my kitchen. I shot straight into the end of his lens as if I might see all the way inside to what made his camera work. The image came out completely black.

CHAPTER NINETEEN

I *got up* in pitch darkness the next morning. The waves
pounded on the sand as I dressed, tiptoed down the
stairs, grabbed an apple from the bowl on the counter,
and slipped out the living-room doors to the sand. I had
taken one picture a day for the last four days. I was
determined to keep taking pictures in this way until
I got one that was perfect, and I had the thought that
sunrise could be it. *Sunrise over Manhattan Beach*, like
Moonrise over Hernandez.

The streetlights along the beach lit up small pools of

light. I followed them north toward the pier. It was cold, and the sound of the waves was so loud that it was amazing to me that in the houses all along the beach, people were sleeping. I came up to the entrance to the pier and noticed a man sleeping against the railing. He had plastic garbage bags wrapped around him for warmth and a grocery cart stuffed with other bags, filled to bursting. Did he have more bags inside the bags? Clothes? Soda cans to recycle and make a few dollars to buy a loaf of bread? I stopped in the darkness and looked around me. There was no one else nearby—not one dog, not one cop, not one late-night reveler trying to get home before the sun.

I knew that you could take a good picture in complete darkness. All you needed was patience. I raised my camera to frame the homeless man and then lowered it. Only one picture was allowed, and it was going to be a picture of the sun. I kept walking out onto the pier. It smelled of seaweed and fish guts and spilled ice-cream cones that had been trampled into the boards beneath my feet. I walked past my favorite bench and out to the end of the pier, where there was the small roundhouse aquarium. Inside there was a shark and a garibaldi, an eel, an urchin, an anemone. I sat at a bench outside their hexagonal home, turned toward the coastline, and waited for the sun. It would rise pink and glorious over the hill of houses that crowded the sand and I would capture it from my perch out on the sea at the exact moment the rays of light burst into view—a postcard-perfect image.

The sky gets light by small degrees. It is night, and then there is a moment when it is something else. I wanted to catch the sun itself, emerging over the houses, so I waited while the light rose. But when the sun peeked over the roofs, I questioned the moment. I waited one beat, then two. And then the sun was there, glaring bright in the sky. "Take it, take it," I told myself, but the sun kept creeping higher, and I kept stalling, and then it was too late. I'd blown it.

I stood and took the camera strap off my neck. I looked at the image of the sunrise I'd just missed and the one of Tommy on the couch in Bailey's studio. I held the camera in my hands for a moment and then I turned and hurled it over the railing. I watched it wheel around in the sky, the strap spinning over and over, the lens acting like a kind of rudder. It looked like a pelican plunging from the sky to scoop up a beakful of fish, but instead of diving and rising, it landed with a sickening *thunk*. Water flew a few inches up, and then there was nothing.

I turned and, empty-handed, walked slowly back home.

CHAPTER TWENTY

I *could have* picked up my Canon G9 and continued taking a picture each day, but something about seeing the Nikon go into the sea made me think that I might never take another picture. I canceled every remaining shoot on my calendar. I spent my days walking along the beach, looking out to sea, staring at the shells and stones and bits of garbage on the sand—balloons and carnations, condoms and plastic bags. I sometimes wondered if my camera might wash to shore one day, the home of barnacles and algae, an oddity that would make some beachcomber think about lost treasure, sunken ships, pirates from a photographic sea.

I told Marisol that we didn't need any dinners prepared just now and spent entire afternoons cooking and baking. I have a book called *The Best Recipe* that examines top recipes for certain classic dishes and then presents a master recipe that takes the best part of all of them. So you turn to "Roast Chicken" and you get a discussion about how to roast the perfect chicken—what temperature, what length of time, whether or not the bird should be turned, whether or not it should be basted, more salt than pepper, more pepper than salt. There is lengthy commentary about the science of chicken roasting, the technology of ovens, the wisdom of letting cooked meat sit before you lean into it with a carving knife. This book, more than any other I know, makes the world seem totally comprehensible.

I spent the next week roasting chickens according to the various directions. I tied up their legs, I slipped garlic cloves under their skin, basted them with butter. We had so much chicken in the house that I resorted to taking platters of meat across the alley to Mrs. Jenkins. The third time I appeared with a browned bird, Mrs. Jenkins laughed at me.

"You're becoming a chicken expert," she said.

"I want to master the art."

"I suppose you have."

"I was thinking I would try some baking next. Strawberry rhubarb with a woven lattice top."

"Make *pfeffernüsse*," she said, but it was more like a command than a suggestion. "I love *pfeffernüsse*, but I've never met an American who can make it correctly. My mother didn't use anise, but everyone thought she did. People tried to copy her recipe, the other women in town, but no one could do it just the way she could. Her secret was dark molasses."

"Cookie baking was competitive in Leipzig, was it?"

"My mother made it so," she said, and then she laughed. "My father, too. He bragged about my mother's *pfeffernüsse* all day long!"

"My mother made amazing pie," I said, "but my father only bragged about himself."

Mrs. Jenkins nodded. "He was brilliant," she said. "It comes with the territory."

"Why?" I asked. "Why is that?"

"To believe you have something to say that the world wants to hear? Whether you're standing on a stage, writing on a page, or putting something on a gallery wall, that takes a lot of ego, and a lot of discipline, too."

*   *   *

I threw myself into the task of making *pfeffernüsse* that would please Mrs. Jenkins. I scouted out the thickest, darkest molasses at a natural-foods store in Santa Monica. I roasted and chopped my own almonds, minced my own orange and lemon peel from organic fruit purchased at the farmers' market, bought a bottle of fine brandy for fifty dollars so that the teaspoonful I used would pack the most punch, and ground the black pepper from fancy Madagascar peppercorns.

I was in the midst of this *pfeffernüsse* frenzy when Bridget called.

"What's with the radio silence?" she asked. "Are you mad at me?"

"I've been busy," I said.

"Work?"

I set down the sifter I'd be using to turn plain flour into clouds of white fluff. "Yeah," I said, "it's been crazy."

"Claire," she said gently, "Harrison called me. He's very worried."

"I let him down," I said. "I was a bad client."

"Because you're not really working, are you?"

"I'm making *pfeffernüsse*. That's work."

"Ah."

"What, there's something wrong with that? You never met a woman who spent a week making cookies?"

"Not a woman as ambitious as you."

"What makes you say I'm ambitious? And don't say that it's in my blood."

"But that's the truth."

"I've resolved to relinquish all ambition. I've decided I'm not cut out for it."

"It's not a bad thing to be ambitious, Claire."

"No, but it's exhausting," I said. "I'm tired of it. Besides," I said, "I'm the mother of an ambitious kid, so that should count for something."

"Doesn't count for squat," she said.

"What kind of a comment is that?"

"It doesn't count for what we're talking about. So make *pfeffernüsse* for a while," she said, "and then pick up your camera again and keep doing the thing you love."

"What makes you think I love to take pictures?"

"I've known you a long time," she said. "It's not a big mystery."

Peter called once that week, as well. "How're you doing?" he asked.

"Great," I said.

"You miss it?" he asked.

"Not a bit."

"So you're coming back soon, then?"

"Peter," I said, "leave me alone."

I could hear Harrison and Bailey whispering around the edges of my baking—they would meet in the hallway and lower their voices; they would stay up at night in the room off the kitchen, talking softly. Neither of them asked me what was wrong, but at the end of the second week when we had no groceries in the house except for the ingredients needed to make a spicy German cookie, Bailey announced that she wanted to go to Driggs, and Harrison said he was ready, too.

"Why the sudden interest in Driggs?" I asked him that night, after Bailey had gone to her room.

"I think it's a good time to scatter the ashes," he said. "I think closure might help you."

I felt the way you feel when you know the people around you think that you are fragile, unsteady, not quite in your right mind. "I don't need closure," I said.

"You seem to be searching pretty hard for something," he said.

"Do you want to know what it is? Do you really want to know?"

He took a deep breath. "Okay," he said.

"I want to make something that feels like an emergency," I said.

He wrinkled his brow, tried to follow my train of thought.

"It's about making art," I explained, "really good art. I've wanted to do that since I was a little girl."

"So why all the baking?"

"It happens to feel like an emergency right now."

"It's hard to watch," he said. "You seem pretty lost. All those chickens. All those cookies. You had a really good thing going."

"You took my career to a whole new level and I'm grateful for it. I know it doesn't look like that right now, but I really am."

He turned to go, and then turned back around to face me. "Why didn't you ever tell me this, about wanting to make art? We worked for months on what you wanted and you never once mentioned anything about art. It was all about the big clients, the big money."

I looked straight into his eyes. "I only just figured it out," I said.

* * *

We flew to Driggs that weekend, and disposed of my dad's remains according to his wishes. We walked from the cabin down to the Owens Bridge and scattered his ashes into the Teton River. The larger pieces of bone floated down and sank to the bottom, where they instantly became part of the rocks and the sand and the reeds. The lighter dust spread out on top of the water, and its oils leached onto the surface and the ashes moved exactly like a cloud, roiling and dispersing as they floated away from us. It made me think of the words on the marker at Ernest Hemingway's gravesite in Sun Valley, Idaho, a few mountain chains to the west. *Best of all he loved the fall, the leaves yellow on the cottonwoods, leaves floating on the trout streams, and above the hills the high blue windless skies.*

Bailey cried, and said she wanted to stay on the bridge awhile to sketch. Harrison and I walked slowly back to the house along the river. The water was so clear that it magnified every pebble and grain of sand. You could see water bugs on the surface, small brown frogs on the rocks at the edges, flies flitting around in a frenzy.

Harrison leaned down, scooped up a handful of water, and examined the bugs that stuck to his skin.

"Hey, Claire," he said, "would you like to learn how to fish? Conditions are perfect."

I looked upstream at the sunlight on the water and the mountains in the sky. "Sure," I said.

We went back to the house and made sandwiches and collected all the gear from the garage—the long rods and the sleek aluminum reels; the mesh vests with a dozen pockets and the tall rubber boots. Harrison carried the box of flies out to the chairs on the lawn by the river. He rigged one of the rods, tied a fly on the end of the line, put on the boots, and waded out into the water. I sat on the chair watching him, thinking that he was already gone—gone to commune with the fish, gone to a place where I didn't know how to follow. But after a few graceful casts, he pulled up a cutthroat about ten inches long, reeled it in, came back on the lawn, and knelt down in front of me. The fish was beautiful—sleek and silver, with a bright red slash near the jaw. Harrison held it firmly in his hand, flicked open a knife and slit the fish's white belly. I made myself look. What I saw was this: a universe of dead flies packed into that trout belly.

"Fish eat flies," Harrison said simply. "Flies are born in the water, then they come to the surface to dry their wings and copulate. They return to the water to lay their eggs. A fish follows this life cycle as if its life depended on it, because, of course, it does. What a fisherman does is he becomes part of this cycle of knowing, and of living and of dying."

I felt as if I were hearing ancient secrets being revealed for the first time. "Okay," I whispered.

Harrison pointed to a row in the box of flies. "Dry flies mimic the adult flies on the surface of the water. Wet flies mimic the larva and nymphs underneath. We're going to put a PMD on your line today," he said, "because it mimics the nymph of the mayfly, which is mostly what that fish ate for breakfast."

I nodded as he reached for a fishing pole. "This rod was your dad's favorite," he said. "It's an Orvis Wes Jordan, made of bamboo. It's probably fifty years old by now, but he loved the feel of it in his hands."

I took the rod in my hands, and felt my heart leap—with nerves, with fear, with gratitude? I don't know. The rod was incredibly light and it seemed as though it was an extension of my arm and my hand, my fingers and my self. My eyes filled up with tears. Harrison stepped closer and wrapped his arms around me. He pulled me in close to his chest and rested his chin on the top of my head. I stayed there for several moments, then turned my face toward the flesh of his neck and kissed his warm skin. He tipped his head and kissed me—a long, slow, deep kiss. "Maybe we should save the fishing for later," he said.

I pulled back. "Not a chance," I said.

We waded into the river, where he taught me the four-count rhythm of the cast, how to flick the rod so that the fly looks as if it's rising from the water, struggling for air. We ate our lunch, and wandered upstream, looking for pools, looking for fish, trying to become part of the river. When I finally hooked a fish, Harrison talked me through what to do—how to reel it in, reach out, and take it in my hands. It was a magnificent rainbow trout, about fourteen inches long, and it had come to me, soft and silent through the water, like a gift. I admired its metallic-blue-green body and the bold line of crimson that ran from its gills to its tail, and then Harrison got out a pair of long-nosed pliers, removed the hook, and placed the fish in my hands. I lowered my hands into the water and watched the trout wriggle free, gather its strength, and dart into a deep pool, where it would no doubt feast on flies until the sun went down.

As soon as we got into bed, Harrison pulled me on top of him and kissed me again in the way that he had by the river. "You're a very sexy fisherman," he said. "I'll commune with you and the fish anytime you'd like."

"You're a good husband," I said, "and a good father and a good person."

The next day, Harrison flew east to go over maple-syrup paperwork, and Bailey and I stayed to work with Alex, who was, of course, ecstatic to meet her. He whisked her into the study, gave a sermon about what was on the wall, explained where things were coming from—which other museums and galleries, which collectors—and made his plea for printing up certain images to fill in certain gaps.

"I don't want to print anything new for the show," she said. "I want it all to be his originals."

"We can't locate all the originals," Alex said. "The owner of *The Devil's Stepping-Stones* won't lend us the print. She won't even let anyone see it. It's a gaping hole."

Bailey looked at me. "So you've been to see Caroline Greer?" she asked. She was clearly surprised that we knew who had the print.

I nodded. "She's adamant. She won't let the original out of her house."

"I'll go talk to her tomorrow," Bailey said.

* * *

In the middle of the afternoon, I snuck into the study and slipped the three slides of the juniper tree back into the notebook where Alex had filed them.

We ate a dinner of packaged noodles and jarred spaghetti sauce, and then Bailey and Alex returned to the study to go over Alex's plan for the retrospective. I took a wool blanket from the linen closet—a red-and-black buffalo-plaid blanket that may never have seen the light of day—and stepped out onto the back deck. It was still quite cold at night, but I could hear the water gurgling in the river, making its case for summer. I sat down on an Adirondack chair and pulled my knees up under the blanket. I thought about what it would be like to die from hypothermia, to die from cancer, to die from drowning, a heart attack, a car accident, starvation, crashing into a tree. I thought of how much resolve it would actually have taken to buy a lift ticket, strap on skis, ride a chairlift, veer toward a tree. There had been a thousand opportunities to turn back.

I closed my eyes and felt the cold in my toes, in my hands, in my earlobes. Sometime after the moon was high in the sky—a small silver crescent pasted against the black—Bailey came out on the deck and gently shook me awake.

"Is he gone?" I asked.

"Alex? Yeah. Why?"

"Caroline has negatives. A series of them that led up to *The Devil's Stepping-Stones*. As long as we're asking for the print," I said, "I think we should ask for the negatives, too."

It was dark. It was hard to see Bailey's face. I couldn't tell if she flinched.

Bailey and I went the next morning to see Caroline. We found her working in the flower beds along the side of the barn, her hair pulled back in a bandanna. When she saw Bailey, she blinked, stood, and took her in her arms like she was a long-lost child.

"I'm in charge of my grandfather's retrospective," Bailey explained. "He left me in charge. Did you know that?"

"No," Caroline said, cutting her eyes at me. "Your mother didn't mention it."

"Did you know he destroyed most of his negatives?" Bailey asked.

"Yes," Caroline said, "I heard that."

"Do you know why?" she asked.

"I have a pretty good idea."

"My mom said you have negatives you believe are my grandpa's," Bailey said. "Would you mind letting us look at them?"

Caroline took off her gardening gloves and led us into the barn. She plugged in the light box and handed Bailey the book of negatives. Bailey carefully looked at each page, peering at their dates. I imagined that she had spent many hours with my dad while he was stalking photos. She probably took her sketch pad with her, and patiently drew while he patiently waited for the right photo of that day. Looking at that series of negatives would be for her like coming home.

But after she scanned the series, she put the book down. "I don't believe that this sequence is natural," she said, "and I'm not even sure this is all his work."

I closed my eyes and took in a breath through my nose.

"You don't believe they are his?" I asked quietly. I wanted to demand to know why she was lying, but I already knew the answer. She had spent every summer of her childhood walking the fields and streams and mountains with my dad. She knew the nature of his genius better than anyone else in the world. She was lying to protect him, and Caroline must have known this as surely as she knew how birds choose their twigs for their nests. She just sat quietly at the table, watching us, a small smile on her lips.

"No, I don't," she said. "This picture of the moon isn't in focus, the tops of these trees aren't in the frame. These aren't his."

I turned to Caroline. "And you?" I asked. "What do you believe?"

She smoothed a strand of her hair back from her forehead. "I believe that Bailey is right," she said.

I just closed my eyes and tried to keep breathing.

"Will you allow *The Devil's Stepping-Stones* to hang in the show?" Bailey asked.

"No," Caroline said, "I'm sorry."

Bailey didn't argue. She didn't even begin to fight. The whole visit had been a performance and somewhere my dad was sitting by a fishing hole chuckling with delight at the ruse he had been able to pull off.

Later that afternoon, I drove into Jackson Hole. The same young man at the camera store handed me my slides and prints. "You should be able to take care of that kind of fuzziness with your Nikon, I should think," he said, nodding at the prints in my hand. I wasn't sure whether to laugh or to cry or explain the whole story to this stranger, but decided, in the end, just to smile and say thanks.

I looked at the photos when I got into the car—new prints of thirty-eight-year-old images, a fresh look at my fifteen-year-old self—and then I got out of the car, went back into the camera shop, and told the stunned shopkeeper that I needed another Nikon.

I drove over to the post office and bought a photo mailer. I slid the photos into the envelope with a note:

> Dear Bridget,
>
> The thing about being a GK is that it can take a long time to accept your fate. In my case, it took fifty-four years. I've bought a new camera (I threw my last one into the ocean—don't even ask) and I'm learning how to fly-fish with my dad's old bamboo rod. I thought you'd like to see these three photos that I took when I was fifteen years old and went out to visit him in Moab. My dad, it turns out, kept

them all this time. I'm not in a legal position to hold on to them, but it would make me happy to know that they're with someone who understands how much they mean to me.

xxoo

Claire

CHAPTER TWENTY-ONE

The next day, back in Manhattan Beach, I went on a run toward the pier and up through town, and came upon the farmers' market. There was a table piled with bunches of stargazer lilies, a table with heirloom tomatoes in a riot of colors, ruffle-edged lettuce, Japanese broccoli, shallots, bok choi, avocados, oranges, lemons, limes. I reached into my pocket and found a ten-dollar bill and a handful of change. I walked up to the flower farmer and stood behind a woman who was buying ten bunches for a luncheon she was having the following day.

As I stood there waiting for her flowers to be wrapped in paper, I noticed the stand next to me. They were selling plums. There were black plums and red plums, speckled plums and small plums, and one hybrid plum they called a pluot. The black plums were an unbelievable shade of dark purple, and I thought that Bailey would probably have a word for it or at least a place where she had seen the color before—in a shadow, in a storm, in the night. The man behind the table picked up one of these dark beauties, sliced off an end, and held it out on his knife for me. I looked at his face. It was tan from the sun, lined, and open, as if he feared nothing in the world. His teeth were crooked and yellowed. His hands were gnarled from years of work in the sun and the dirt. If I'd had my camera, I would have taken his portrait. I stepped out of the flower line, took the piece of plum he offered, and slipped it into my mouth. It was sweet and cool.

"I have ten dollars," I said, and handed him the crumpled bill. "I'd like some of each."

He smiled—a smile that lit up his whole face—and handed me back a huge bag full of fruit.

I walked home. When I stepped off the beach path into the lane by our house, Mrs. Jenkins was sitting at a table under an umbrella, sipping iced tea.

"Good morning, Mrs. Jenkins," I said.

"Back in town again, are you?" she asked.

I nodded. "We've just come from burying my dad in Driggs."

"I'm terribly sorry," she said, and reached out her spotted hand and rested it on mine.

"I've been to the farmers' market," I said. "Would you like some plums?"

"Of course!" She reached in and took five plums from my bag. "You should reserve some to make jam," she said. "There's no better jam than plum."

On Saturday morning, I made jam, and before the jars had cooled, I took two over to Mrs. Jenkins's house. I rang her doorbell, but she didn't answer. I walked around to the side of the house and knocked on the kitchen door, but there was no reply. Her housekeeper didn't work on Saturdays, so I eased open the door. I can't explain why I felt a sense of dread, but I definitely felt it—something hard and dark in the normally sunny seaside air. When I stepped inside, I saw her sitting at her cherry dining-room table—the Queen Anne antique she'd brought back from Germany one summer when she sang Wagner's *Ring* and was the toast of Berlin. Her face was toward the ocean, her back to me.

"Mrs. Jenkins?" I asked, and walked through the

kitchen, and through the passageway toward where she sat. She looked like she might be praying, with her head bowed to the front, and I tried to recall if she had ever mentioned anything about praying or church or even God. Her right arm was hanging straight down at her side, and there was a plum on the marble tile right underneath it. The plum looked alive—like it was moving—and when I stepped closer I saw that it was covered with ants. A trail of ants marched from the plum toward the dining-room window.

I took a step forward and saw, then, that she was not praying or sitting or eating.

She was dead.

I thought, suddenly, about the movie *Stand by Me*, which I saw at a theater in Greenwich Village not long after my mother died. It was based on a Stephen King story about a group of young boys who are both attracted to and repelled by the dead body of a boy their own age. It wasn't a horror story—just a tale about life and death in a small town—but it horrified me all the same. When it was over, I sat in the theater and cried for the boys' lost innocence, for the brutality of life and the finality of death, and even though Harrison kept asking me what was wrong, I couldn't answer; I didn't know what it was about that movie that had gotten to me in such an elemental way. But standing there in the presence of Mrs. Jenkins's body, I felt something of the same thrill and something of the same repulsion that those boys in the movie felt.

Mrs. Jenkins had been dead for some time—maybe all day, maybe all night and all day—because her skin was very gray and waxy. Her ankles were swollen to the size of her calves, and her fingers were puffed up like sausages. She had taken a seat at her table with a small white Limoges plate, a small Henkel knife, and one of the plums I had given her the day before, and she had gotten no more than a slice into it when she had died, perhaps of a stroke or a massive heart attack. It appeared that there hadn't been one moment of trauma. She was just sitting there, the knife laid across the plate, the plum dropped neatly beside her, a hundred or more people a day going by outside her dining-room windows on bikes and roller skates, in bikinis and yoga pants, walking dogs, heading to the volleyball courts, moving with that lightness that always comes from being alive and at the beach.

"Harrison," I called out, thinking, somehow, that he might hear me. The sound came out of my mouth as a small rasp.

I turned and ran back through the kitchen, across the walkway, and then burst through the door of our house and raced up the stairs to where Harrison was taking off his running shoes.

"Mrs. Jenkins is dead," I blurted.

"What do you mean, she's dead?"

"She's just sitting at her table. She's dead."

We ran downstairs, out the door, across the walkway, and through Mrs. Jenkins's kitchen, to the place where the ants continued their plum-flesh feast. Within seconds, Harrison was on the phone to 911. The call made no sense to me, because 911 was who you called when you needed help fast—when someone was drowning, when someone was choking, when someone had swallowed a fistful of pills, but I didn't know whom you called when someone was clearly long past needing help.

When he hung up, Harrison directed me to go home and get his cell phone, which had Mrs. Jenkins's son's phone number on it. I was glad to have something to do—a small chore, a bit of direction. I raced home and found the phone in our closet. I grabbed it, and then turned and went back for my camera. Something in my brain flashed an urgent message about the need to record Mrs. Jenkins's scene of death, to capture something essential that had happened there, to preserve that one slice of time in which all time stopped. I raced for the camera and then returned to Mrs. Jenkins's dining room.

Harrison stepped outside to get a signal on his phone, then dialed Mrs. Jenkins's son. I raised my camera and looked at the plum, the trail of ants, the plate with the knife laid across it, the waxy gray hand hanging totally limp, and then I turned the lens toward Mrs. Jenkins's face. I zoomed in on the elephant wrinkles around her eyes and focused on the place where her hair came out of her scalp like a small, spare forest, her parched and colorless lips. If I had only one chance to take a photo of this scene, which one would it be? Which one photo would say something about what had happened here—this life, this death? I veered back toward the plum, soft and black, a thing whose aliveness was still so visible, and whose purpose—to be eaten—was so clear. I positioned it half out of the frame, with a trail of ants trailing off to the far edge of the picture, and clicked the shutter.

Later that night, Harrison came into the bedroom where I was watching *The Daily Show*. He handed me a shot glass of tequila—the same drink he'd brought me the night my dad skied into a tree. It was the Espolón Añejo, a dark amber liquor with a vanilla aftertaste. We had it for the first time at a bar in Madrid that boasted over a hundred different kinds of tequila, which we thought we might work our way through one night. When it was clear we weren't going to make it very far, we asked to try to the most expensive tequila in the house. The bartender told us that the Espolón was so finely distilled it was incapable of causing a hangover. Some people keep Advil and Ambien on hand for headaches and nights of bad news; we kept the Espolón.

"Thank you," I said. I took a sip and felt the burn. It felt shocking and transformative.

"You okay?" he asked.

I shrugged. "It's a hell of a way to die," I said. "Sitting there by yourself."

"Facing the ocean, eating a fresh-picked plum, with probably not one second of realization of what was happening?" Harrison asked. "I say that's a hell of a good way to die."

"I don't know," I said. I kept thinking about the people who were sitting on the beach in Phuket reading a book and sipping lemon water, and who heard the sound of the tsunami coming and turned and saw it rushing forward and instinctively knew that there was no way they would ever be able to outrun that much water, or to swim to the surface, or to float to safety. Was that a worse way to die? Or what about the girl in the photo that my dad kept on his desk for thirty years—the Vietnamese girl crouched in the dirt with a torn rag of a dress who gazed with total innocence just moments before she was shot dead? Was that even worse still? Maybe our whole notion of what death was and how it worked was so wrong as to be laughable. Maybe the more you are aware of your own death, the better, somehow, it is on the other side. Maybe people with total awareness that their time on earth is over get to start the next life ahead of everyone else.

Harrison sat down on the bed, then pushed me forward and slipped behind me so that I was cradled between his legs. I leaned my back against his chest and took another sip of tequila.

"What did you take a picture of?" he asked. "Her hand?"

I thought about denying that I had taken any pictures. I thought about saying something about feeling that it was important to record the facts of the scene. "The plum," I said.

He reached over and picked up his shot glass. I heard him gulp, suck at his teeth, exhale. "Is it any good?"

I leaned forward, twisted around so that I could see him. "I don't know," I said. "I haven't looked at it."

"It's probably the best shot you've ever taken," he said.

"Why would you think that?"

"Because it's the first time you ever took a picture without thinking."

CHAPTER TWENTY-TWO

There *was a* story not long ago in the *Los Angeles Times* about a group of motorcycle riders who cruise around the state to attend the funerals of fallen soldiers. They started out coming to protect a family whose son's funeral was being picketed by war protesters, but they ended up feeling so uplifted and empowered by the experience that they began to send members to every funeral of every fallen service person in California. They show up—this band of scruffy-looking guys on motorcycles, with their long beards, their black helmets, and their solid purpose—and they bring an unmistakable air of dignity to the events.

I saw them riding in a parade in honor of a young man who had been on the football team here. The parade was following the casket from the funeral party to the football field, where there was to be a memorial service. The Patriot Riders, as they call themselves, held American flags as they rode, two by two, behind a horse-drawn carriage carrying the casket. I was sitting in my car at a stoplight, waiting for the police to let us through. I had the impulse to jump out of the car and hop onto the backseat of one of those choppers, but I didn't. I kept on doing whatever it was I was doing that day. The same thing had been true with every other funeral I had ever attended. I always started out thinking that I might start adhering to some religion's rituals, because the whole idea of a funeral is so moving and the stained-glass windows are so ethereal and the hymns resonate in your bones in a way that I like, but the thought never lasts past the next Sunday.

Mrs. Jenkins's funeral was held at All Saints Beverly Hills, an Episcopal church that sits within a stone's throw of Rodeo Drive, on a prime corner lot shaded by towering palm trees. The pews were filled with distinguished-looking men wearing cashmere suits and muted ties, with ladies wearing St. John knits, with people in shoes that had been polished, or purchased, for the occasion. These were people who knew how to dress.

The service was a very formal affair. It followed the stiff Episcopal liturgy, with readings and prayer and a brief homily about singing a new song to the Lord. After the minister spoke, the bulletin noted that a Mrs. Tamara McSweeney would be singing "Summertime" from *Porgy and Bess*. I watched as an African-American woman, very small and frail, with a wave of white hair, raised herself up from a wheelchair and began to make her way up the steps at the front of the church. Two tall, stately black men held each of her arms as she climbed the red-carpeted stairs and stood in the elaborately carved wooden pulpit. They moved two steps back and sat in the stalls normally reserved for the choir. I found myself worrying about how she would sing. I worried that her voice would be too soft, that it would crack, that she wouldn't get through the piece. But Mrs. Tamara McSweeney turned on the little light, and she turned on the microphone. She placed her hands on the lectern in front of her, opened her mouth, and began to sing in such a way that no one could take their eyes off her. Her voice was no longer smooth or deep or sure, but you could tell that it had been at one time. You could hear in each note the long life this woman had led, the many things she had seen, both good and bad. It was the voice of a woman who was offering her dear departed friend the best that she had to offer—her testimony of this life, her hope for whatever life might come next, her love, her loss. It seemed to lift all of us up so that we floated there, above the cardinal-red carpet, like angels.

It was definitely an emergency.

I began to cry. I hadn't counted on crying. Mrs. Jenkins had been old, and she had lived a good life, and the only thing I could say I would miss about her was the occasional friendly chat when she was in town and I was in town and we both happened upon each other. But she had lived in a way that I found to be beautiful. She liked plums and summer storms and the simple fact of sharing stories through song.

I cried because in order to take pictures with the same kind of conviction, I didn't need magic and I didn't need stardust and I didn't need permission from my dad. All I needed was to believe that I could do it. And sitting there in that church, in that light, surrounded by that music, I suddenly, finally, believed that I could. Harrison, dry-eyed beside me, fished a handkerchief out of his pocket and handed it to me with a sweet smile. I wanted to believe that he knew exactly what I was crying for.

* * *

On the way out of the church, we were stopped by the plug of people at the door. I found myself standing right next to Tamara McSweeney, whose wheelchair was parked near the baptismal font. I smiled at her. She smiled back.

"Your tribute was lovely," I said.

"I sang that song in 1943 when *Porgy and Bess* opened at the Pantages," she said, "and people would stand and applaud us for twenty minutes. Sofia Jenkins came to hear us for five straight nights. She sat in the orchestra, in a different dress each night. That's how we met."

"She came five nights in a row?"

Tamara nodded. "She said she was studying it, breaking it down."

"Is that a fact?"

"Oh yes, indeed. I heard her sing it at Tanglewood the summer of 1958. People are probably still talking about that afternoon. George Gershwin stipulated in his will that only African-American singers could be used when the full production was performed. I bet old George might have changed his mind if he'd been there that day to hear Sofia sing."

"She was my neighbor," I said. "She was a very good neighbor."

Tamara smiled. "She was a very good woman."

The crowd surged forward, and we moved out of the church and into the sunlight.

I went out to the beach the next morning, and onto the sand. The waves were breaking very small and shallow, and the ocean almost seemed like a lake. There were washes of rocks and shells every hundred feet or so, as if the calmness of the water had coaxed the treasures to come out. It was quite windy, and there were only a few people walking near the water, jackets drawn against the cold.

I walked just at the edge of the waterline, forcing myself to trust that the wash wouldn't come up and lick my shoes the way it does in winter. I looked for dolphins, but saw nothing breaking the surface of the water. I looked at the pelicans flying in their lopsided Vs overhead, and remembered a time out on Santa Cruz Island. We'd hiked along the cliffs over Potato Harbor and those Vs of pelicans had glided in the air exactly even with us, perhaps ten feet from where we walked. When we stopped and held our breaths, we could hear their wings flapping—an ethereal, rhythmic *whoosh*.

Ahead of me, I saw an object sitting on the sand.

Waves washing over it, but it sat there, unmoving. It was the size of grapefruit, the shape of a Hershey's Kiss. I stepped closer, and when the next wave washed out, I saw that it was an enormous conical shell. I waited for the next wave, then dashed out and grabbed it. I quickly set it on the dry sand, bottom side up, and waited for an angry crab to emerge. Nothing happened. I turned the shell over and said, "Oh my God" out loud to no one but myself. A spiral ridge curled around it from base to tip in perfect symmetry. Smooth nubs on the spine were rubbed raw and a glimmering jewel-like whiteness shown through the brown-green skin. I looked around, because it was too hard to believe that no one else had seen this unusual shell, that it had emerged from the sea at exactly the right moment for me—and only me—to find it.

I picked it up and kept walking. The shell felt heavy beyond reason in my hand. It felt as if it were vibrating, and I turned it over, and looked, again, for a crab. I blew into the opening and felt cool air come out on my skin. I took it home, washed it, dried it, and placed it in the center of the mantel above the fireplace.

"What's that?" Bailey asked. She had just come down the stairs.

"A shell. I just found it on the beach,"

"You found it?"

"Just sitting there."

"Wow," she said, "it's amazing." She walked over and picked it up. I flinched and made a move as if she were still a small child, as if she couldn't hold such a fragile thing in her hands without damaging it.

"Mom," she said, and held the shell out, balanced on her flat, outstretched palm. "You can trust me."

I thought of the seagull painting and of how Bailey had destroyed it. She was part of a long history of artists who had done the same thing. Paul Cézanne destroyed his own canvases during bouts of depression. De Kooning destroyed his in his search for identity. Monet destroyed some of his to prevent them from being seized by creditors. Georgia O'Keeffe once stacked all her paintings in a room in order to evaluate them, and she destroyed them all because she judged them to be derivative of someone else's style. The artist's path can be twisted and strange. Maybe destroying the seagull painting had been essential to Bailey's journey as an artist. Maybe my touching the tip of a brush to it had merely been the catalyst for something bigger.

"I know I can trust you," I said, and my head was full of the reality of my relationship with Bailey—of the raw fact of how much I loved her and how much she loved me, and of how we were bound together by things that we seemed unable to talk about and unable to escape. I wanted to put all that into words, but realized that I didn't need to. All of it was contained in the shell she held so carefully in her outstretched hand. "I wish," I said, "I had figured that out a long time ago."

She looked at me. "You mean before the seagull?"

I shook my head. "I definitely should have trusted your genius as a painter," I said, "but I also should have trusted your genius as a person."

"That's deep, Mom."

I laughed. "Yeah," I said, "but it's true."

"I wouldn't worry about it," she said. "I mean, you trust me now, right?"

"I do."

Bailey turned the shell over in her hands and examined the pearly whorls. "And I forgive you," she said. "So we're good."

I would have hugged her, but she was still holding the shell. I could see fine grains of sand sprinkled across her palm like sugar. She turned it over and examined the pearly whorls in the light. "I'm going to paint this," she said, "for you."

Tears filled my eyes and spilled down my cheek. "Thank you," I said, "but what about your other work? Are you done with those paintings?" I hadn't looked in her studio for weeks. I hadn't even been tempted.

"They're practically painting themselves," she said.

"Tommy's the perfect muse. He's so beautiful and soulful."

"You also know exactly what to do with the muse," I said.

She shrugged. "I just put the brush onto the canvas and let come whatever is going to come."

"You don't think? Plan? Agonize?"

She shook her head. "Sometimes," she said. "Mostly I just paint."

CHAPTER TWENTY-THREE

several months later we flew to New York for the opening of Bailey's show. There was a cocktail reception on the Friday night, but none of us could wait that long to see what the paintings looked like framed and hanging on the big creamy walls. We arranged to meet Antonio, the gallery owner, on Thursday morning at nine, but when we arrived at the Chelsea storefront, the doors were locked. We stood on the sidewalk with our faces nearly pressed against the glass door as we tried to see the paintings and how they looked on the walls and how they filled up the space.

I had my Nikon and Bailey and I took turns looking through the zoom to see if we could see any better that way.

"Just hold on," Harrison kept saying.

Bailey squealed with impatience. She was like a six-year-old waiting for her birthday party.

I couldn't stand the anticipation. I walked a few steps to the café next door, where people were eating omelets and blueberry muffins the size of grapefruits. I read the dessert menu posted in the window: almond biscotti dipped in Valrhona dark chocolate, mango sorbet with coconut crisps, crème brûlée with fresh raspberry coulis. I imagined exactly the way each of them looked—the precise way that the almonds in the biscotti winked as if they were knowing eyes, the way the coconut stuck out of the crisps like wisps of wayward hair, the way the coulis pooled around the crème brûlée as if the dessert were a little island in a sea of summer.

When I turned to walk back to the gallery, the city rose up in the background—a grid of windows, a constellation of spires. On the left, there were cars on the street and knots of people on their way to work, to school, to the doctor, to the gym. And on the right, alone on the sidewalk, spotlighted perfectly by a shaft of light as if they were on a stage, was a group of three people. There was the handsomely dressed gallery owner holding open the door, holding out his arm to invite Harrison and Bailey inside. But Harrison had stopped and put his hands on Bailey's shoulders as if to hold her in place, hold her down, while he leaned in to deliver a message—to tell her, perhaps, how proud he was of her, to tell her how lovely she looked, how lucky she was, how much she was loved, or to remind her to remember this moment for the rest of her life: the moment when she had created something that inspired people to stop and take a moment out of their busy lives to feel what it was like to be alive.

I saw something there in that scene on that street in New York, something magnificent and powerful that I had never seen before. I lifted my camera and pressed the shutter, and in a split second I captured my history as well as my future: here was a father loving a daughter in a way I had never been loved, but instead of being separate from that reality, I was part of it. I was part of the circle. My camera made it so.

she meets Harrison. What is the story of *your* inner artist?

3. What is the single most magical creation you've ever made with your hands? Can you remember the feeling you had while you were making it? What happened when you showed it to the world?

4. The story begins to spiral out of control when Claire tries to fix a speck on Bailey's seagull painting. If you are a mother, did you ever cross a boundary like that with your child? If you are a daughter, did your mother ever step over a line like that with something of yours?

5. Have you ever been jealous of someone you love?

6. Claire's discovery of her old photos in her father's archives has a profound impact on her. Were your parents the kind of people who held on to objects from your childhood for sentimental value or did they throw things away? If you are a parent, what are your habits in terms of family keepsakes?

7. Have you ever caught a fish? Describe what that was like.

**Eight Conversation Starters for Mothers,
Daughters, and Other Creative Folk Who May
Want to Discuss This Book with Their Friends**
Plus
**Two Behind-the-Scenes Moments
from the Author**

1. The question of what we inherit—both physi-
    cal objects and intangible characteristics—runs
    through the entire story. Have you ever inherited
    something that threw your life off balance—a
    house, a photograph, a family business, or a habit,
    passion, or belief? What have been the pluses and
    minuses?

2. Bailey's artistic impulse is nurtured throughout
    her life, whereas April's is largely shut down until

8. Claire learns that her father learned to see the world better by slowing down and taking one photograph every day. Do you do anything to slow down your own busy life? Do you practice yoga, play the piano, go on walks?

Behind-the-Scenes Moment #1:
Photographs in My Mind

My dad, Dr. Roderick Nash, was a professor of environmental studies at the University of California at Santa Barbara for nearly thirty years, and is the author of many books, including *Wilderness and the American Mind*, an intellectual history of what wilderness means to this country. I had the privilege of spending a great deal of time with him in the American West. We ran rivers, climbed mountains, camped in the desert. There is a well-known saying (attributed to several different sources) that when we go into the wild we should take nothing but pictures, leave nothing but footprints, kill nothing but time—a plea to walk lightly on the earth that has ominous undercurrents in these days when the word *footprint* is most often spoken with the word *carbon*. The odd thing is that, although there were occasionally professional photographers along with us on our expeditions (most memorably, a guy named Valentine who snapped a photo of me and a friend standing under a waterfall that ended up as a spread in *Sunset* magazine), we mostly didn't take pictures of the spectacular places we visited. We just swam in the water, played in the mud, felt the warmth of the sun and chill of the rain. In my current life as a mother and a writer, I don't get to be out in those wild places as often as I used to, and some of them don't even exist anymore. They have been flooded by dams, plowed under by bulldozers. But they are seared into my memory, powerful and indelible.

Behind-the-Scenes Moment #2:
Me and Jim Brandenburg

About five years ago, there was a feature story in *National Geographic* about a wildlife photographer who took a picture a day and only a picture a day for 365 days. The photos were reproduced as small thumbnails in a grid in a spread, and I was mesmerized by the idea of them, and the layout of them, and the eerie beauty of them—and then I closed the magazine and forgot about them. When I began to write *The Only True Genius in the Family*, I remembered the *National*

Geographic piece and tried to track it down. I looked in boxes in my garage, on shelves at the library, on the magazine's website, on the Internet. Time after time, I entered different combinations of search words in Google, thinking I'd turn it up, but I got nothing. Year of pictures, year in pictures, year of wildlife, 365 days of photos, nothing. It began to drive me a little bit crazy. I gave the picture-a-day-exercise to the characters in my book, though I wasn't very convinced about the veracity of it, and then one day something magical happened. I was at my friend Paula's house discussing what kinds of paintings my character Bailey should make. Paula was pulling art magazines and books off her bookshelf and piling them up for me to take home and study. She pulled down a book called *Chased by the Light* and said, "Was this the inspiration for your picture-a-day thing?" I glanced at the book, whose cover was a photo of fall leaves on a pond, and said no; my inspiration had been a magazine article that had a lot of wolves in it. Paula said, "I have no idea where I got this book anyway, so you can have it," and she threw it on the pile. Once I got home, I read the introduction to the book and gasped. These were the photos! This was the guy! It turns out that the exercise photographer Jim Brandenburg set for himself was to take a picture a day from the autumnal equinox to the winter solstice. It was a picture a day, and it was wildlife and wilderness, but it was never a year. It also happens to be a gorgeous testimony to art, nature, and the human spirit. I was so relieved and grateful and amazed and inspired to hold that book in my hands.